"You gotta love a heroine who is not only addicted to Nut Goodies but also tells a newbie how to eat one."

—*Saint Paul Pioneer Press*

"Nut Goodies serve as an ideal metaphor for Lourey's writing . . . sweet, nutty, evocative of the American Heartland, and utterly addicting."

—*The Strand*

"Mira is the strength of the book. She has a unique voice, full of irreverent humor . . . I couldn't help rooting for [her]."

—*All About Romance*

"*May Day* starts the action rolling with a clever mystery and some snappy writing . . . These pages are filled with fresh dialogue . . . an offbeat mystery."

—*In the Library*

"Jess Lourey writes about a small-town assistant librarian, but this is no genteel traditional mystery . . . She flees a dead-end job and a dead-end boyfriend in Minneapolis and lands up in Battle Lake, a little town with plenty of dirty secrets. The first-person narrative in *May Day* is fresh, the characters quirky. Minnesota has many fine crime writers, and Jess Lourey has just entered their ranks!"

—Ellen Hart, author of the Jane Lawless mystery series

"Lourey knows her turf."

—Peter Handel, *Pages*

"Jess Lourey writes a light-hearted murder mystery, and she writes it well."

—Who-dunnit.com

"This trade paperback packed a lot of punch . . . I loved it from the get-go!"

—*Tulsa World*

knee
high ^{by}
_{the}
fourth
^{of} july

OTHER BOOKS BY JESS LOUREY

May Day

June Bug

FORTHCOMING BY JESS LOUREY

August Moon

knee
high by
the
fourth
of
july

Jess Lourey

MIDNIGHT INK
WOODBURY, MINNESOTA

First Edition
First Printing, 2007

Book design and format by Donna Burch
Cover design by Lisa Novak
Cover illustration © 2007 by Yuki Hatori / CWC International, Inc.
Editing by Connie Hill

Midnight Ink, an imprint of Llewellyn Publications

Library of Congress Cataloging-in-Publication Data

Lourey, Jess, 1970–.
 Knee high by the Fourth of July / Jess Lourey. — 1st ed.
   p.   cm. — (Murder by month mystery)
  ISBN: 978-0-7387-1035-8
1. Minnesota—Fiction. I. Title.
PS3612.0833K58   2007
813'.6 —dc22   2007016941

This is a work of fiction. Names, characters, places, and incidents are either the product of the author's imagination or are used fictitiously, and any resemblance to actual persons, living or dead, business establishments, events, or locales is entirely coincidental.

Midnight Ink
Llewellyn Publications
2143 Wooddale Drive, Dept. 978-0-7387-1035-8
Woodbury, MN 55125-2989 USA
www.midnightinkbooks.com

Printed in the United States of America

For Dr. Holly Hassel, my first and best editor.

ACKNOWLEDGMENTS

First, I'd like to thank my poor TV reception. If not for a pitiable selection of channels, I would write much less. Second, I'd like to extend a heartfelt thanks to my lackluster social life. Because of those endless nights at home, *Knee High* was able to see the light of day. Third, and most importantly, thank you to my mom for coming to watch the kids so I could write, thank you to my dad for keeping everything working in my house so I could concentrate on more important stuff, and big love to my children, who inspire me to evolve and grab all that life has to offer.

I've also been remiss in my earlier novels in not thanking the people of Battle Lake, who are good sports about the fun-poking and murder-creating I do in their beautiful town. If you've never been to Battle Lake, go. It's worth the drive, and Chief Wenonga is just as sexy as you think he is.

ONE

It was the first Thursday in July, the hottest month in Minnesota. The thermometer was busting my hump at a moist 86 degrees, and it wasn't even 8 AM. The Channel 7 news, the only station that came in clearly at my double-wide in the woods, was predicting the hottest July in history. The humid, sticky weather made the whole state feel like a greenhouse, or the inside of someone's mouth. As a direct result, people who had to work were cranky, people on vacation were ecstatic, and crops were growing like a house on fire. Locals said that if the corn was knee high by the Fourth of July, it would be a bumper crop. We were two days shy of that date and the corn was already shoulder high on a grown man. That strangeness should have been a warning to us all.

I stepped out of the shower into the sauna of my bathroom, wrapped a towel around my wet hair, and crossed the house to flick on the morning news. The droplets of water on my naked body felt deliciously cool against the heavy morning air.

Rinnng.

A phone call while the sun is still pinking the horizon never bodes well, particularly for someone like me who was lucky enough to have been within two feet of one fake corpse and two real ones in as many months. I let down my hair and rubbed it, stirring up the spicy smell of rosemary ginger shampoo.

Ring.

I tossed the towel over the back of a chair and reached for a pair of tattered jean shorts.

Ring.

I threaded the button fly and reached for a midnight blue tank top with a built-in shelf bra to rein in the booblets.

Ring. My answering machine clicked over, and whoever was calling hung up. *Must not have been important.* I unclenched my shoulder blades and went to brush my teeth. I squeezed out a pea-sized glop of Tom's of Maine cinnamon toothpaste, trickled a little water on it, and started scrubbing.

Ring.

Shit. I ran through a list of people I knew who could be dead or hurt, of money I owed, and of anyone who might be mad at me.

Ring.

The sigh came from the bottom of my soul. I was gonna have to answer that phone. A few years ago, I could have ignored it, but the older I got, the less reliable my denial mechanism became. I wondered what other cruel tricks my looming thirties had in store for me. That simultaneous wrinkles-and-pimples one was my favorite so far.

"Hello?"

"Mira James, please." The male voice had an East Coast inflection and a monotone delivery, as if the speaker were reading off a card.

"Speaking."

"Hello, Ms. James!" I could almost see the exclamation point quivering in the air. "How are you today?"

"I'm fine. How are you?"

"I'm good, thank you! Tell me, Ms. James, has love found you?"

I pulled the cordless phone back from my head, looked at it, found no hidden cameras, and pressed it back against my ear. "What's this about?"

"It's about helping you find love. Are you single or married?"

"Who is this? Are you asking me out?"

I heard a rustling of pages, a quiet second of reading, followed by tinny laughter. "Why no, Ms. James. I'm calling to find out if you'd be interested in joining Love-2-Love, the new online dating service from Robco. We have thousands already entered in the system, and one may be your soul mate!"

Cripes. I needed a soul mate like a monkey needed a bikini wax. "Yeah, no thanks."

"Registering is free and easy, Ms. James! Save yourself from a lifetime of loneliness. Let me read you a testimonial from some of our newest customers."

"Do you know it's 7:30 AM in Minnesota?"

"This is from Becky Rafferty, West Virginia: 'Before Love-2-Love, dating was a tedious process that involved many hours of picking through unsavory men in the hopes of finding one good egg. Now, Love-2-Love chops that time in half!'"

"Nothing personal. I know this is just your job, but I'm really not interested."

"Check out what *Dr.* Alan Rotis of Pennsylvania had to say. 'Like you, I was suspicious of online dating. That was before I met my beautiful wife, Lora. Thanks, Love-2-Love!'"

I wondered what hellacious karma debt had placed my name on this phone list. Had I smashed a bunny on my way home from work? Cut off a nun in traffic? Accidentally killed someone? Ooh. Maybe this was payback for not pursuing a relationship with the post-operative transsexual professor I had been set up with in May. Man, somebody somewhere was keeping a close eye on the score. "I have to go to work."

Another riffling of papers. "I understand, Ms. James. You're happy without love in your life, with no one to take romantic walks with at night or to smile into your eyes as you wake up. Could I give you our web address in case you change your mind and decide you don't want to die alone?"

"Sure."

"Do you have pen and paper?"

I had my car keys in one hand and the doorknob in the other. "Yup."

"OK, it's www.love2love.com. The '2' is written as a numeral."

"Got it. Bye."

"Thanks. And rememb—"

I clicked the "end" button, tossed the phone on the couch, let out my calico kitty, Tiger Pop, and Luna, my German Shepherd-mix foster dog, and was out the door. Nobody likes to be told they're in for a lifetime of loneliness, but for me, the issue was especially painful. I had formally filed love in the junk drawer of my mind two months ago, right about the time my erstwhile boyfriend, Jeff Wilson, turned up murdered in the Pl–Sca aisle of the Battle Lake Library, a bullet hole drilled through his forehead. There's nothing quite like finding your man dead at work to turn a gal off dating for a spell.

The downside to this out-of-sight, out-of-mind philosophy of mental health and romance was that when I finally found someone worth opening the junk drawer for, it was going to be messy. In the meanwhile, I really *was* happy with myself, and it didn't hurt that I had a good, detachable showerhead and reliable water pressure. I also had been attending a Community Education class early Saturday mornings taught by Johnny Leeson, local horticultural hottie. The next class was called the Second Sowings of Lettuce and Beets, but what was more pressing was Johnny's curling golden hair, strong hands, and the smell of sun-heated black dirt and spicy greens that followed him. Something about his organic quality turned me into an idiot in his presence, so I admired from a distance, keeping my junk drawer tightly closed.

When thoughts of Johnny weren't enough to keep me company, I took emotional isolation to a whole new level with Chief Wenonga. Aah, the Chief. Twenty-three well-sculpted feet of dark alpha male forever guarding the shores of Battle Lake. He was the perfect man, if one overlooked the blatant racist stereotyping and the fact that he was a giant fiberglass statue. If he had been in the Love-2-Love system, I might have joined. The Chief visited many a dream of mine, all strong and silent, sporting a full headdress, six-pack abs on a half-naked body, tomahawk in one hand, and the other hand raised in a perennial "How."

The Chief, or at least his statue, had been in Battle Lake for exactly twenty-five years this July. The Battle Lake Chamber of Commerce had originally commissioned the figure as a tribute to the flesh and blood Chief Wenonga, an Ojibwe leader who gave the town its name in 1795 in honor of a fierce battle with the Sioux. The Chief was my favorite part of summering in Battle Lake. Or at least that's what I would call what I was doing if I were rich. Since I wasn't, I called it house sitting for my friend Sunny and holding down one job running the Battle Lake Public Library and another as a reporter. The newspaper I worked for, the *Battle Lake Recall*, came out every Wednesday and sold for fifty cents.

Matter of fact, I had just gotten promoted and now wrote my own column, "Mira's Musings," which was a nice addition to the weekly recipe feature, "Battle Lake Bites," that I also penned. My new column ran on the back page of the *Recall*. There was even a tiny black-and-white photo of me that ran with it. It was so fuzzy that my long brown hair looked dark gray, my freckled skin looked light gray, and my gray eyes looked black. It didn't really matter because as far as I was concerned, no headshot was going to show my best qualities—my brain and my ass.

I was granted "Mira's Musings" because news seemed to find me in Battle Lake, first in the shape of Jeff, whose lifeless body I discovered in the library in May, and then again in June when I uncovered the mystery of the disappearing jewels on the shore of Whiskey Lake. Ron Sims, the editor for the *Recall*, hadn't asked for any specific content when he assigned me the weekly column ten days ago, but I assumed he wanted me to write about murder and money when I could find them and gossip and garage sales when I couldn't.

It was because of this position as star reporter that I was on my way to the Chief Wenonga Days final planning meeting. Every July, to celebrate the man who had named the town and the coming of his statue a couple hundred years later, Battle Lake hosted a three-day festival. It was always scheduled the weekend closest to the Fourth of July so the town could double-dip on the tourists. Wenonga Days perennially included Crazy Days and a street dance on Friday; a kiddie carnival with turtle races, a parade, and fireworks on Saturday; and a bike race, pet and owner look-alike contest, 5K run, and all-town garage sale on Sunday. The planned revelry this year would be extraordinary, though, because the Chief statue was twenty-five years old. The festival happenings weren't in the hands of the citizens of Battle Lake, however.

The Wenonga Days final planning meeting was only a formality designed to make the entire town feel involved without letting them actually have any say. Kennie Rogers, the town mayor and resident busybody, was the mastermind behind the festivities, and she wanted to keep it that way. I knew for a fact that she had organized the entire weekend last summer, including booking a country group for the street dance and getting local high school bands and organizations like the Girl Scouts signed up for the parade. Normally, she opened the final planning meeting to the public two weeks before Wenonga Days so that there was a semblance of town involvement without enough time to actually change anything. This year, however, Kennie had been out of town until late yesterday to receive some hush-hush training, and she refused to allow the Wenonga Days pretend planning to begin until she returned. I suppose I could have skipped the meeting, particularly because the paper wouldn't come out until Wednesday, three days after Wenonga Days was over, but I had promised Ron I would cover it.

I sniffed at my armpits as I drove my rusty, light brown 1982 Toyota Corolla to the meeting in town and wondered if the unrefined rock deodorant I had picked up at Meadow Farm Foods outside of Fergus was going to hold back the floodgates. The lush hardwoods lining County Road 83 looked tropical, but there were no birds singing. It was too crazy hot. I propped my left foot on the top of my driver's side door and splayed my blue-painted toenails, redirecting the tepid morning breeze pawing at my wet, half-combed hair. The other foot was holding the gas pedal at a constant sixty-two miles per hour as I navigated the snake curves of Whiskey Road with only my right hand on the wheel. This was the coolest I was going to get all day.

I pulled up to the stop sign at the intersection of County Roads 83 and 78. On my right was Larry's grocery store, across the street was Stub's Supper Club, and to the left was the old granary. I turned north on 78, also called Lake Street, and drove the two blocks to the Battle Lake Public Library. The yellow brick building was barely ten years old and an incongruity in a tiny town. William T. Everts, a man who made his fortune in the lumber industry and a beloved mainstay in Battle Lake until his death a decade ago, had bequeathed his entire estate to create it.

The library was located on one corner of Lake and Muskie. First National Bank, Area Lakes Dental, and a temporarily abandoned building that once housed Kathy's Klassy Klothes occupied the other three corners. I had noticed some activity in Kathy's Klassy windows lately, and word on the street was that soon a quilting shop—or maybe a kwilting shop—would occupy the building. Alongside each of these cornerstones were knick-knack and antique stores, a bakery, two hardware stores, a drugstore, a post office, a Lutheran church, and various service offices—chiropractor, accountant, real estate agent. It was a full-service small town with something for everyone.

I parked my car in the "Librarian's Spot" behind the library and hoofed it the half block to the Chamber of Commerce office for the final planning meeting. The sun beat down on my dark hair like a blow torch, and I wondered if blondes stayed cooler in the summer. By the time I got to the Chamber, sweat droplets were tickling my lower back and gathering in the spot where my cleavage would be if there was any fairness in this world. As it was, the sweat trickled to my belly button, unimpeded by my A-cups.

The gathering was scheduled to last from eight to ten, but I would need to ditch a little early to open the library on time. The Chamber of Commerce shared a squat, one-story brick building with the post office. The main room was designed to hold up to forty people for town meetings, and today, it was full to bursting. I shook my head, amazed that so many townspeople had a stake in the events of Wenonga Days, twenty-fifth anniversary or not. Didn't everyone know the planning wasn't for real? A loud but calm female voice broke through the din.

"I understand that. I'm just saying that to dedicate a town and a weekend to celebrating the objectification and stereotyping of a whole race of people is a blatant exercise of hegemonic privilege, no matter how much business it brings to Battle Lake."

The people in the crowded room murmured their affront, both at the content and length of her words. I couldn't see the speaker, and I didn't recognize her voice. It had a strange lilt, like she was singing the middle of the sentences. I elbowed closer to get her in view.

"We'all are *honoring* the Chief." Kennie Rogers was not hard to find. She was at the front of the room, one hand on the podium and the other on her hip. Her clothing was muted, for her: platform flip flops, black and white calfskin capris, a white pleather fringed belt that distracted from her overspill of skin in the thigh/genital area, a suede vest over a yellow tank top not up to the challenge, a peacock-feather choker, what appeared to be teepee earrings, and I swear she wore a beaded headband. She had curled her brittle, white-blonde hair around it, sort of like a living stage starring her hairline. Her makeup reinforced the tacky Indian theme started by her clothes—nude lipstick, maroon blush troweled just under her pale cheek apples to imply stark cheekbones, the same color on each side of her nose to make it look fierce, and shades of brown eye shadow caked above her fake eyelashes.

Welcome to Battle Lake. I jostled my elbows some more, still unable to spot the woman who believed it was worth her time to argue about the objectification of American Indians with a thirty-eight-year-old Norwegian dressed like Porn Pocahontas.

"I recognize that you feel you are honoring the Ojibwe with your festival," the voice broke in.

I finally caught sight of the speaker, standing two rows from the back. She was wearing a taupe pantsuit, strawberry blonde hair pulled back in a loose ponytail, revealing a strong-featured, make-up free face. She looked about my age, late twenties or early thirties, and gave an overall impression of capability. I could tell by the lines around her generous mouth that her normal facial expression was a smile. This morning, however, she was all grim business. She pushed back her jacket sleeves to continue, and I was surprised by the Celtic tattoos on each of her wrists belying her otherwise conservative appearance.

"However, to promulgate the stereotype of Indians as savages, to celebrate capitalism with your 'Crazy Days' on what used to be consecrated ground, and to disregard the historical significance of the Battle Lake conflict with a kiddie carnival and parade is disrespectful to Native Americans, and to those who respect individual human value." Her words were clipped, and I got the impression she was dumbing down her speech for this audience.

Her points ignited a louder buzz throughout the room, but Kennie drowned it out. "What did you'all say your name was?"

"Dr. Dolores Castle. I am a professor of Native American Studies at the University of Wisconsin, and I represent the People for the Eradication of American-Indian Stereotypes."

PEAS. I had always wondered if groups came up with the acronym and then a name to fit it, or vice versa. In this case, I assumed they thought up the name first because the green vegetable was not really associated with crusading strength. Asparagus, I could see. Peas, no.

I turned my attention from Dr. Castle to the people watching her. Most wore a Mask of Bewildered Anger, the official expression of rural Minnesotans confronted by liberal progressives. There was no way she understood the depths of institutionalized stereotyping she was up against. Battle Lake even had a tradition of substituting Indian "warriors" (basically Shriners in face paint, fake leather pants, and moccasins) for clowns at the Wenonga Days parade. I knew the town wasn't trying to maliciously malign anyone, but I also knew how the celebration would appear to the rest of the world. It was only five years ago that Battle Lake finally replaced the high school mascot, a stereotypical Indian warrior chief they called The Battler, with a bulldog, and that change had been hotly contested.

Dr. Castle continued. "We don't want you to stop your festival. We are just asking that you rename it and remove all Indian caricatures from your region, including Chief Wenonga."

The whispering crowd suddenly went whip-silent.

"Remove…" My voice cracked as I went from observer to participant in light speed. Suddenly, she was hitting a little too close to home with this talk about taking my big man away, and it slapped me right off my judgmental pedestal. I raised my voice to get her attention. "You mean remove Chief Wenonga *actors* from the *parade*, right?"

"I mean remove the statue of Chief Wenonga from the town."

My stomach plummeted and the room got a little hazy as a net of panic encircled me. Then, for a nanosecond, I saw the beauty in this idea. He could come live with me. We wouldn't have any misunderstandings about whose job it was to take out the garbage or arguments about my emotional inaccessibility. Oh no. Just clear expectations. He'd be there when I needed him, always. And then my brain fluttered back to reality. The Chief wasn't mine. If he left Battle Lake, I'd never see him again, and neither would anyone else. Suddenly, the audience of nearly fifty people erupted with wild talk and outraged looks. Dolores Castle held her ground, hands crossed serenely at her waist.

"Silence!" Battle Lake Head of Police Gary Wohnt pounded the podium with a gavel he got from I don't know where. The crowd didn't stop talking, but they hushed their voices. Gary had that effect on people. He was big like a bull, with dark eyes and hair, and his itchy silences could elicit confessions from the dead. I didn't like him, which made sense: he was pompous, he applied Carmex like his life depended on it, and he always caught me at my worst, usually around dead or seemingly dead bodies. What I didn't understand was why he didn't like me.

"Are there any other general objections for the Wenonga Days Festival before we continue with the planning?"

I think Wohnt meant this as a segue and not a serious inquiry, but to his chagrin, Les Pastner stood up. Les was a card-carrying local militia guy, and he had run against Kennie in the last mayoral election on the platform of "Les Is More." He had lost.

Les owned the Meat and RV Store right off of 210 where he sold used Winnebagos and wild game that he smoked in-house. When business was slow in the winter, he worked odd carpentry jobs around town, bitched about the government, and spread rumors that the police left him alone because they knew he was sneaky and fast. Except for running for mayor last summer, he mostly blended in. Apparently, though, Les' activism was cyclical, and we were witnessing his annual blossoming. He stood in the center of the Chamber, a'tremble in his fatigues, all five foot two inches of him tensed. His close-set features, which had always made me feel like I was talking to the three finger holes of a bowling ball, seemed darker than usual.

"I been quiet for too long, and I ain't gonna be quiet no more!"

I could see Les' eyes get disorganized, and I wondered if he had missed a dose of some medication. He puffed himself up, which only served to make his face redder and his features deeper-set.

"We don't honor the white man! Nuthin' against the Indians, but it's about time the white man gets some. That's all I'm saying. You don't see no statue of any big white man in Battle Lake. We need to get rid of Wenonga, get us a big white man, and have White Man Days in July!" And just like that, Les deflated and fell back into his seat.

The room underwent a collective headshake. Who would have thought anyone had the time to object to a once-a-year festival in a tiny town, and here we had two serious protestors, one who was even articulate? This was the last thing I had expected from the meeting. The ironic part was that Dr. Castle and Les kind of wanted to get the same thing out of this meeting—no more Wenonga. I considered, as a concession, informing Les that every day was White Man Day in Otter Tail County, but I didn't want to lose my hair in the angry mob scene *that* would create.

I scanned the front of the room. Gary Wohnt appeared to be on an inner mental voyage, and Kennie's mouth was opening and closing like a wide-mouth bass on land. Somebody needed to pull this meeting back on track, and soon, because I needed to open the library and didn't want to miss the good stuff. I was about to step up when a reedy voice cut through the crowd.

"Bullshit. You two are singing in the key of crap." Mrs. Berns, my favorite octogenarian, was pointing a bony finger each at the doctor and Les. "As long as we have Chief Wenonga, we're having Wenonga Days, and a twenty-plus-foot statue ain't going nowhere. So stop with the malarkey and get on with the planning. If I don't get back to the home by 9:30, I don't get my snack."

Mrs. Berns had been a peripheral player in the last two adventures I had been swept up in. She had even turned out to be a pretty good informant considering she lived in the Senior Sunset, the local nursing home and not exactly what you'd think would be a hotbed for clues. Turns out the old-homers were a force to be reckoned with and had the best dirt in town. Sometime last month, Mrs. Berns had also created and then applied for an assistant librarian position at the library, and she was making me proud I had hired her. Despite a randy streak that often found her dancing suggestively and wearing see-through blouses and no bra, she was a good worker and a practical woman, which was my favorite kind.

Mrs. Berns' interjection yanked Kennie out of her reverie and back into her Southern denial mode. "I do declare, it's time to plan a party!" PEAS, Les, and all things unhappy were dismissed. Reality got in line behind Kennie.

That was my cue to leave—the library was waiting. Surprisingly, I enjoyed the job. If you had asked me when I was a girl what I wanted to be when I grew up, I wouldn't have said "librarian." Actually, I probably would have said "cat," but I've always been a dreamer. Currently, I lacked the degree and the skills to ever be a real librarian, but under the circumstances, the town was happy to have me. And I was happy to be here, mostly. The library perfectly joined my love of organization and books.

I liked the job less on days like today, however. My shift was a whirlwind of clearing out paperwork, answering a mad influx of tourists' questions ("If I like Janet Evanovich, who else would I like?" "Can I check out the magazines?" "Do you give library cards to out-of-towners?" "Where would I find that purple children's book about the bear?"), and shelving books, leaving me no time to draft "Mira's Musings" or write my recipe column or even to find out what came of the uproar at the pretend planning meeting. In fact, I was forced to stay late to catch up on my daily paperwork and didn't leave the library until 8:00 PM.

When I stepped outside the air-conditioned chambers, the hot, muggy air hit me like a blast from a kiln. My hair wilted to my head like a skullcap, and the last bit of energy was broiled out of me. The tar parking lot felt soft and sticky and reeked of cooked gravel and blistering motor oil as I walked to my car. I was smart enough to pull my tank top over my hand before grabbing the metal door handle. Once in, I rolled down all four windows, moved the emergency blanket to cover the volcanic Naugahyde that was the front seat, cranked the radio, and headed for home.

When I pulled up to the mailbox at the end of my mile-long driveway seven minutes later, I realized I was too tired to eat, forget about calling around to find out what had come of the planning meeting today. I parked the car in the shade of the lilac bushes, near where both Luna and Tiger Pop were resting. Luna thumped her tail and Tiger Pop opened one eye when I petted him, but that was about all the welcome home I got.

In hand I had a bill from Lake Region Electric; a flyer for a new store called Elk Meat, Etc. opening in Clitherall, the tiny dot of a town six miles east of Battle Lake; and a birthday-card-sized white envelope. My birthday had been in May, and there was only one person I knew who sent cards two months late. My mom. There was no return address, but the post office stamp said "Paynesville." Yep, it was from my mom. I thought about opening it, but decided I wasn't up for it tonight. I loved my mom, but our relationship was not comfortable. We'd had a minor breakthrough since I'd moved to Battle Lake, but I was moving gingerly within the relationship. I think I was still mad at her for not divorcing my dad when she had the chance.

Instead, she stayed married to him despite his drunkenness throughout my entire elementary and middle school years, and through my first two high school years, until he was involved in a fatal car accident at the end of my sophomore year. After that, I was known as Manslaughter Mark's daughter and fled to the Twin Cities as soon as I had my high school diploma in hand. That worked out for a while, until I started doing my best imitation of my dad, getting drunk every night and letting my life slide. Moving to Battle Lake had been designed to shake me out of following in his footsteps, and I was proud of how I had been doing since May.

At least I was until I had received the letter from Dr. Lindstrom last month, asking me to return to Minneapolis to be his research assistant in the U of M's Linguistics department. When I read that letter, I sort of felt like a failure, spinning my wheels in a small town while life and a real career passed me by. So I didn't read that letter very often, though in the back of my brain I knew I'd need to make a decision about staying in Battle Lake or moving back to Minneapolis by the end of the month, as he had requested.

I dropped my unopened mail on the table inside the front door, changed Tiger Pop's and Luna's water, dropped some ice cubes into their bowls, refilled their food, coaxed them into the stifling house, and apologized for neglecting them all day. They both plopped down on the cool linoleum near the refrigerator, and I considered joining them. The ant creeping across the floor nixed that idea. I tossed my jean shorts and tank top over the back of the couch and crawled naked onto my bed, a fan pointing at my head. The air it was moving around was so scorching that I would have been better off rigging up a flamethrower.

I slept on top of the sheets, except for my feet, which I always covered in bed. Seeing a *Roots* rerun on TV as a child had affected me to the point where I couldn't leave my feet vulnerable for fear of having them chopped off as I slept. I knew the sheets wouldn't stop an ax, but they made me feel safer, and after two months in Battle Lake, I needed all the reassurance I could get.

———

I woke up seven hours later with a layer of sweat covering me like a salty wool blanket. An icy shower and a quick breakfast of whole-grain Total with organic raisins, and I was on my early way to meet another oppressively hot day. I knew my Wednesday "Mira's Musings" column was going to be somehow related to the Wenonga Days planning meeting, so I needed to find out how it ended and get a draft of that out before I opened the library. Besides my regular filing, ordering, and organizing duties there, I wanted to take down the Fourth of July holiday decorations—the library would be closed on Saturday and Sunday—and replace them with generic summer ornamentation. Somewhere in there I also needed to find a recipe "representative of Battle Lake" (in Ron Sims' words) for that column. My to-do list for the day was getting as stifling as the hazy July air.

The fertile smell of the swamp I passed by on the gravel tickled my nose, and I could hear frogs singing in the sloughs. The sun was scratching the horizon when I turned right onto County Road 78, just up the street from the Shoreline Restaurant and Chief Wenonga. I had chosen this route because driving past Chief

Wenonga on my way to town seemed like a natural way to get my (mental) juices flowing.

I was just turning onto the tar when a red tank zoomed over the hill and aggressively hugged my Toyota's bumper. Whoever it was had their brights on, unnecessary in the bright dawn and making it impossible for me to see their face in my rearview mirror. I was pretty sure it was a guy with a small penis, though. My feet twitched to tap my brakes, but it was too early in the morning to trade my safety for my pride. I pulled to the right to let the Humvee pass and glared at the silver-rimmed tires as they raced past me and my puddle jumper. Feeling cranky, I drove the last mile into town, cursing tourists and gas-guzzling army vehicles. I was moving on to getting mad at the color red when I crested the hill right before the Shoreline.

The restaurant's parking lot was peppered with a sprinkling of early morning fishers in town for the excellent eggs Benedict and hash browns. My temper cooled a little as I thought of good food and the fact that I was just about to say a great good morning to my big fiberglass man. I leaned forward in my seat so I could spot him a millisecond sooner. Just beyond the brown roof of the Shoreline, I made out Chief Wenonga's cement stand, with four bolts poured into it. I didn't remember seeing the bolts before, and a beat later, I realized why. The bolts held Chief Wenonga up, one each in the front and back of his feet. Now that he was no longer there, the bolts were obvious. Someone had stolen Chief Wenonga.

TWO

I SCREECHED INTO THE parking lot, threw myself out of the car, and ran to the Chief's stand. I touched the four bolts, cool and wet with morning dew, and looked around frantically. Where were the police? Where was the ambulance? Why wasn't anyone doing anything? I could see the fishers eating their eggs through the picture windows of the Shoreline, their eyes happy, their mouths talking, as if someone important to us hadn't just disappeared. Cars drove past on 78. Waves lapped at the shore of Battle Lake, and the sun was rising steadily through the morning mist. How could the world go on as if nothing were wrong? I was struck with an image of me slapping the Chief's photo on the back of milk cartons and attaching posters to interstate semis.

I swallowed a deep breath and squeezed my hands into fists. There must be a rational explanation for this. People don't kidnap ginormous fiberglass statues. Probably at the meeting yesterday it had been decided that the Chief needed a cleaning, and workers had quickly driven him to some fiberglass statue detailing shop.

Or maybe they had decided to add a "Find the Chief" contest to Wenonga Days. Or maybe…an icy finger traced a shiver down my spine. Maybe, just maybe, Les had decided to do his own part to promote White Man Days, or PEAS was pulling a stunt of PETA proportions.

My horror turned to anger, and then, thank God, to embarrassment. My Chief Wenonga obsession had clearly gotten out of hand. I made a mental note to find a new, more reliable fixation, and in the meanwhile, to visit the local coffee shop, the Fortune Café, to see what I could find out about the Chief's new location. I wiped my dew-covered hands on my shorts and marched back toward my car. When I reached for the door latch, a swath of red caught my eye. It was on my faded cut-offs, and it was the smear I had just left with my hand. Since when was dew red?

For a moment, I entertained the notion that the Chief had bled when he was removed from his posts. It made sense, in Crazyland—the posts were the only thing I had touched. It was the fiberglass stigmata. Then, good sense crept into my head, followed immediately by fear, and they both slid down my neck and back like cold oil. I had real blood on my hands.

THREE

My legs propelled me back to the cement stand, and bending down on shaky knees, I examined the bloody post more closely in the hazy, early-morning sunlight. I saw what my eyes had missed earlier in my Chief grief. At the base of the post was a gory patch of dark hair the size of a silver dollar, still adhering to the chunk of scalp it had sprouted from. Where, I wondered, was the rest of the person? It was time for the law. I climbed into my car and screeched the mile to the police station.

It was a Friday morning on a major holiday weekend, and I was sure the local police department would be open for business. I was wrong. There were no Crown Vics parked out front, and Wohnt's customized blue and white Jeep was nowhere in sight. A quick peek in the door confirmed that the place was empty. Hmmm. I could always call 911, but I needed to figure out how to report a chunk of a scalp next to a missing fiberglass Indian without sounding loony.

A quick review of the facts verified this was impossible, but I drove to the public phone outside Battle Lake Gas anyway. I had never dialed 911 before, and I was nervous, like I was auditioning.

"911. What is your emergency?"

"Umm. I'm in Battle Lake, and we have a big statue here, Chief Wenonga? Well, he's missing, and there's blood on the posts that held him up, and it looks like there is some hair and skin there, too."

"Human hair?"

Am I Quincy now? "Looked like."

"What is the location of the blood and hair?"

"Right off of Lake Street in Battle Lake, on the other side of town if you're coming in from the south. Next to the Shoreline restaurant in Halvorson Park."

"Are you there right now?"

I suddenly felt like I was being watched. I looked around and saw a handful of cars driving past on 78, and on the other side of that, Timmy Christianson shaking out the rugs inside the door of Larry's supermarket. Immediately behind me and on the other side of the front glass window, the Battle Lake Gas clerk was reading *The National Enquirer* and smoking Pall Malls. "No."

"Your name?"

"Linda Luckerman." The lie came quickly. If I had learned anything from my stint in Battle Lake, it's that you don't look for trouble because it'll find you just fine on its own, thank you.

"We'll send a car right out. Can you be waiting for us at the site?"

"Yup." Lie number two.

"Thank you, Ms. Luckerman." Click.

When I replaced the phone, I was revolted to see a line of blood crusting on my hand. Now that I was removed from the visual horror of the scalp, I was convinced that it was human. The hair attached to it had been thinning, about two inches long, and even though the edges were crusty with blood, I could see it had been recently trimmed.

I stepped inside the air-conditioned gas station to wash my hands, scrub the front of my shorts, and buy a Nut Goodie. I needed to clear my head. I started to feel better immediately after paying for and palming the candy, and I slipped around the side of the building to chow it while sitting on my haunches, out of sight. As the creamy chocolate and nuts slid down my throat, it became immediately apparent that I needed to hightail it out of the Battle Lake Gas parking lot because my 911 call could be traced. When I bit into the hummingbird-food-sweet maple center, it occurred to me that it wouldn't hurt to wipe my bloody prints off the phone on my way out.

I snuck back around to the gas pumps, eyed the clerk who was still reading *The Enquirer* with his back to me, yanked some paper towels from the dispenser, and surreptitiously wiped the pay phone's handset and number pad. I chucked the last piece of chocolate into my mouth and the green, red, and white wrapper into the garbage and decided to amble down to the Fortune Café and drink some coffee as if nothing was amiss so as best to gather clues. It was still entirely possible that the Chief's disappearance was unrelated to the bloody scalp at his base, and if I kept my mouth shut, I might overhear some relevant gossip.

The Fortune was across the street and a block and a half down from the library. Sid and Nancy, the owners, had moved here from the Cities and bought and renovated the charming, Victorian-style dwelling a few years earlier. The downstairs housed a full-service bakery and coffee shop made up of four rooms—the large, flour-dusted kitchen; the main sitting room where you placed your orders and could sit at one of the five tables; the bathroom with a hand-lettered wooden "shit or get off the pot" sign inside; and a smaller all-purpose room off the main one with couches, book-shelves filled with mystery and romance paperbacks and some nonfiction, two desktop computers with Internet access, and board games like Scrabble and Monopoly. The sprawling upstairs was Sid and Nancy's home.

The welcoming jingle of the door and the aromatic wash of fresh-roasted coffee and candied-ginger scones woven into the cooled air called up a Pavlovian response in me. I found myself relaxing, even downgrading the Chief and the human scalp from scary urgent to important as I glided to the front counter, nodding at the handful of patrons I knew.

"Green tea or decaf mocha, Mira?"

Sid had foregone her usual flannel shirt in favor of a camo-green tank top, and she was growing out her mullet into a softer, feathered bob. I didn't know what was at the source of her outward feminization, but I thought it might have something to do with all the issues of *Maxim* she had been reading at the library lately.

"Today's a straight mocha kinda morning, Sid. Do you have any bagels left?"

"For you, we have bagels. Onion or honey oat?"

"Honey oat with olive cream cheese, please." It was feeling like a two-breakfast day. I fiddled casually with the plastic-flower-topped pencils at the front counter, all seven of them stabbed deeply into a flowerpot of French-roast coffee beans. "So, any news in town?"

Sid smirked. "Do you mean the hullabaloo at the planning meeting yesterday? Nancy and I are thinking of naming a new drink after Les. We'll call it The White Man."

"What's in it?"

Sid laughed. "Milk, with a side of fish-shaped sugar wafers. Or whatever you want. It's Battle Lake."

"You hear any other buzz in town?"

"Just the hum of your thighs as tomorrow's Community Ed class looms large. When are you going to ask that Johnny Leeson out, anyhow?"

That set me back a step. I realized that rumors traveled fast as greased ice in a small town, but I had only confided in my friend Gina about my crush on Johnny, Battle Lake's resident hot, hot, hottie. If everyone knew I had a crush on him, did that also mean they knew about my fixation on Chief Wenonga? I shook my head in lieu of an answer, traded Sid a five for the bagel and coffee, and headed to a computer. I set myself up at the Dell that had a direct sight line to the front door.

My plan was to fake researching my next recipe while keeping one ear on the talk. All the important news came through the Fortune, and I'd soon be able to find out what was up at Halvorson Park, former residence of one Chief Wenonga. My favorite pretend work was recipe hunting for my column, so I dug in, hoping the clicking of the keyboard would soothe me. Mostly, I relied on Internet searches using the keywords "weird recipes." I fired up the computer and sipped my chocolate coffee, cinnamon-laced whipped cream sticking to my upper lip.

Today, I varied the keywords in Google by entering "weird Midwest recipes." The first hit was for French-fried skunk. What got me about this so-called recipe was all its assumptions—that a person could get their hands on two dead skunks, know how to skin and debone them, and successfully remove the scent glands before cutting the carnivores into "French-fry shaped" pieces. After that, it was a pretty straightforward fried food recipe, except that you needed to boil the skunk for forty minutes and ladle off the scum before plopping the pieces in an egg, milk, and flour shake. Then, voila! You were ready to fry.

It occurred to me that quite a few people in town, Les Pastner among them, might already know this recipe, so I kept searching. Then, just like that, the magic instructions splashed onto my computer screen: "Find a Man Casserole." The ingredients were tried-and-true. Two cans cream of mushroom soup, half a box of elbow macaroni, half a cup of milk, a can of tuna (the better to bait your man with, I imagine), one can of green beans, and half a cup of pearl onions. Boil the macaroni until soft, drain, and then bake the whole works at 375 degrees for 50 minutes, pull out, cover in a fish-scale pattern with whole, plain, non-ruffled potato chips, and cook for another five minutes or until chips are browned.

This town was missing one giant man and most of another, littler one, and maybe, just maybe, if all of Battle Lake cooked this casserole the same night, we'd find the Chief and the guy-minus-a-chunk-of-scalp who disappeared with him. If nothing else, it would offer the locals some variety from fried panfish and frozen pizza.

I was emailing a copy of this recipe to Ron Sims, my editor, and enjoying the calming feeling I get when I finish a job, when the door to the café crashed open. In fell a red-faced Jedediah Heike, son of the owners of the Last Resort, a popular summer spot on the north side of town. Jed was an amiable stoner in his early twenties, medium height with stringy arms and legs swinging off his skinny body, his happy head topped off with a mop of curly brown hair. He had befriended me when I moved to town in March and was overall a sweet and harmless guy, if not the sharpest tool in the shed. I foresaw him living with his parents his entire life, a regular Battle Lake fixture. However, because he spent most of his time smiling and nodding his head, he didn't possess a lot of credibility in town. "Chief Wenonga is gone!"

I groaned. Of all the people to spread the news. And now I could surmise the worst, that the Chief wasn't supposed to be gone. He had been stolen. Sid came out from the back room. "What's that, Jedediah? Are you OK?"

"The Chief Wenonga statue. It's missing. It's gone!"

"You ever hear about the little boy who cried wolf, Jeddy?"

The handful of patrons in the café laughed good-naturedly at the joke, but Jedediah's face fell. His brown doe-eyes landed hopefully on me.

I sighed and stood up, walking into the main room. "It's true. I drove by there this morning. Chief Wenonga is gone."

Jed grinned like a football fan watching an overtime game who's just discovered a fresh, whole Dorito in the crack of his recliner.

"Why didn't you say anything?" Sid asked me. Nancy came up behind and put her arm around her partner.

I shrugged, feigning innocence. "I thought they took it as part of the Chief Wenonga Days deal. You think we should call someone?"

"Ya!" Sid reverted to a good Norwegian brogue in times of stress. She dialed the Battle Lake Police Department, got through to someone, and in minutes, a Crown Vic sped past, siren blaring. I didn't know if they were responding to my 911 or Sid's call, but the results were the same.

Most of the café customers were on the street by this time, gawking in the direction of the Shoreline. I shut down my computer, bundled up my uneaten bagel in a napkin, and jogged down the road. There was safety in numbers, and now I could snoop up close while the whole town milled about. Besides, I wanted to be there when Gary Wohnt discovered that somebody had stolen a twenty-three-foot heirloom on his watch.

FOUR

Jed tagged along behind me. I tried to ignore the huffing and puffing caused by his ganja-restricted lungs, but when he started to suck in air like a vacuum with a hole in its bag, I slowed my sprint to a fast walk. I was dying to reach the scene of the crime in time to hear what the police made of the scalp, but not at the expense of Jed's life.

"I bet some kids stole the Chief." Wheeze.

"Maybe, Jed. You OK?"

He puffed himself up a little but quickly realized he needed the air elsewhere and instead ran his hand through his sweaty curls. His black Phish T-shirt was plastered to his scrawny chest. It wasn't even eight in the morning yet, and already it felt like Hell's kitchen. "Oh, ya. I'm fine." Wheeze. "I had a feeling something like this was going to happen. There's street gangs forming in town."

We were coming down the hill. Battle Lake was glittering in the hot morning sun to our right, and a cop car was glittering to our left. Battle Lake Police Chief Gary Wohnt was leaning on his open

Jeep door, radio in hand. I could hear his voice, but we were too far away to make out his words. "Where'd you hear that?"

Jed hitched up his belt and pulled a pack of Jolly Ranchers from his back pocket. He offered me a watermelon one and popped it in his own mouth when I shook my head. "I'm not sure where. You know, I might just be thinking of a movie I saw. It's hard to keep that stuff straight."

I shook my head. Jed was so transparently dorky that it was hard not to like him. "You want to go talk to Wohnt with me?"

Jed's face went white except for the bong-shaped ring of acne around his mouth. "Nah. You go on ahead."

I smiled at his back as he disappeared into the crowd, his shoulders hunched around his ears to make himself less visible. I strolled to Wohnt's car, reaching it just as he clicked off the radio. "Secure area, Ms. James," he barked.

"Need help putting up the police tape?"

His Poncherello-style reflective sunglasses were impenetrable as he grabbed the yellow tape from his trunk and strung it around the elm trees despondently circling the Chief's former position. The empty stand the Chief had stood proudly on for a quarter century stood out like a tombstone. We had lost our leader.

In this part of the state, erecting twenty-three feet of kitsch to honor a person, event, or creature was not out of the ordinary. In fact, if a person happened to be cruising around in space and looked back at Earth, and if the only discernible shapes from that distance were continents, oceans, and gargantuan statues, Battle Lake and its environs would stand out like a white-trash Stonehenge.

There was a reason so many statues ended up in the area, and it was called tourism. The population of any Minnesota town situated near a lake (which is every Minnesota town) swells in the summer as hordes of white-backed men come to fish and drink, long-suffering women come to shop and drink, and kids come because they're forced to. This built-in audience serves as the perfect justification for creating oversized replicas of everyday phenomena, a dioramic playground for Bob's Big Boy's fiberglass family.

The tiny town of Battle Lake, population 747, had more to offer than Chief Wenonga, of course—there were the walleye honey spots, antique shops, an ice cream and candy parlor, cozy resorts, and bait stores—but it was its position at the center of a maelstrom of strange effigies that made it the *crème de la crème* of tourist stops. Oh, yes. The glorious and disturbingly sexy twenty-three-foot fiberglass statue of the Chief had just been the beginning. Eighteen miles to the west of the Chief lay the town of Ashby, where the world's largest coot overlooked Pelican Lake. The ten-foot-tall concrete mud hen was so heavy that the wings had to be supported by a metal brace.

Fifteen miles to the west and north of the coot sat Fergus Falls, where the world's biggest otter kept an eye on the shore of Grotto Lake. He was forty feet long from his black nose to his rump of pure poured concrete. Vergas was farther east and served as the residence of a twenty-foot loon. North of that was the world's largest turkey, twenty-two feet of fowl fiberglass, in Frazee.

South and east of that, in the town of Ottertail, rested the biggest dragonfly in the universe. If you followed the back roads farther south, you'd end up in Alexandria, where you could get your picture taken between the welcoming fiberglass thighs of Ole

Oppe, better known as Big Ole. He was a twenty-eight-foot-tall Viking, and although he was taller than Chief Wenonga, I think the Chief could take him in a fair fight. Driving northwest back toward Battle Lake through Vining, you would find everyday objects rendered colossal in scrap metal along Highway 210—a huge clothespin, a titanic toe, a supersized square knot. There was more, but you get the idea.

Every bit of this deranged splendor was flaunted in or within sixty miles of Battle Lake, situated in Otter Tail County in west central Minnesota, a land unto itself where there's one boat for every six residents. My three months living here had proven that Otter Tail County had all the makings of a Midwestern Bermuda Triangle, and the fact that Chief Wenonga had gone missing just underscored that notion.

By the time Gary Wohnt had come full circle with the yellow and black tape, a crowd had gathered and two more police cars had pulled up, one county and one Battle Lake. Kennie Rogers was in the back of the Battle Lake car, behind the cage. When the driver failed to let her out immediately, she began pounding on the inside of her window. The crowd chuckled, but had the sense to do it facing away from her.

"For heaven's sake, didn't your mama raise you right?" Kennie demanded of the young officer, once she was released. Her Southern accent was eternally puzzling, given that she was born in Battle Lake and had only moved out of town for two semesters about twenty years ago to get her cosmetology degree from Alexandria Technical College, all of forty-five miles away.

The offending officer, a baby-faced newcomer named Miller, had to steady her by her elbow as she adjusted her patriotic stovepipe hat, which rode three inches taller than the crowd. It did a lovely job of accenting her glittering, Roaring '20s–style can-can dress with the metallic fringe. The dress itself was charming, if completely out of place, and several sizes too small for Kennie.

She ducked her flustered, red, white, and blue bedecked body under the crime scene tape and marched right up to Gary Wohnt. I was at the front of the crowd and heard every word they said.

"What in the hay-ell is goin' on here?"

Gary Wohnt fished a tiny, black-white-and-yellow tub of lip balm out of his front shirt pocket and twisted off the top. He frosted his lips like they were devil's food cake before answering her. "Wenonga is gone."

"And I'm not stupid. Now that the introductions are over, why don't you tell me what in the hay-ell is goin' on here?"

That was when the Otter Tail County officer came up, a 35-mm camera around his neck, and slipped a latex glove onto each hand. "Chief Wohnt, Ms. Rogers." He nodded to both and proceeded to the statue's base.

"You know Brando is supposed to be here any minute," Kennie hissed to Wohnt. "And you pulled me out of rehearsal for this?"

I perked up my ears. Marlon Brando? And what sort of rehearsal was Kennie at, wearing that outfit?

"I know," Wohnt said. He capped the Carmex and slipped it back into his pocket.

Kennie threw her hands up in exasperation, nearly knocking off her Uncle Sam hat. She stormed over to the county officer, who was photographing the post where I had seen the scalp earlier today. "What are ya'all takin' pictures of?" She asked, her voice sweet like honey.

"Ms. Rogers, I'm going to have to ask you to leave the secured area. Officer Miller? Will you please escort Ms. Rogers out of the cordoned area? And grab the fingerprinting kit from the backseat of my car. I've got a good set here."

The crowd was buzzing behind me, but I couldn't hear it over the sound of my stomach crashing to the pavement. That good set of fingerprints was very likely mine. I had stepped right into it again.

FIVE

I FELT GREEN. IF they found my fingerprints on Wenonga's post, mixed in with the blood, I would be a prime suspect in whatever statue-stealing, man-scalping extravaganza had taken place here. And I knew from experience that the local law would not be sympathetic to my case. I could confess to Wohnt right now about having touched the post, but the fact that I hadn't told him right away would make me appear guilty.

I threaded my way through the crowd, trying to put distance between the cops and me, and ran smack dab into Dr. Castle. Today she was dressed in conservative espadrilles, an ankle-length peasant skirt in muted browns, and a beige silk tank top. Her hair was pulled back into a bun, and her face was pale except for the sunburned tip of her nose.

"Whoa," she said, smiling kindly as she stepped back a pace. "See something up there you didn't like?"

I smiled weakly. "I think I ate a bad breakfast."

She nodded sympathetically. "I saw you at the town hall meeting yesterday, right?"

"Me, and a bunch of angry citizens. You know the Chief is gone, right?"

She stared at the space where his head used to be. "They know who did it?"

I studied her face as she stared at the sky. Her eyes were a light green, almost translucent, and she had a light dusting of freckles over her cheeks and her peeling nose. The police didn't know who had taken the Chief, but I knew who *didn't*—me—and I also knew who would gain from doing it: Dr. Castle and Les Pastner. Since it would be in my best interest to pin that tail to a donkey other than myself, post haste, I'd best start asking questions. I swallowed my bile and held out my hand.

"They don't. I'm Mira James, by the way." She shook my proffered hand, warmly and confidently. "I work for the *Battle Lake Recall*. Mind if I buy you a beer tonight and pick your brain for an article I'm working on about Wenonga Days?" I winced at my own choice of words, considering that there might be a little brain on the Wenonga base.

"Sure. Like we say in PEAS, all press is good press."

"How about the Rusty Nail at 7:00? It's right on Lake Street, a block or so down from Stub's."

"It's a plan." She winked and moved toward the front of the crowd as Jed stepped back toward me.

"This is wild stuff, Mira." His normally bloodshot eyes were glowing, and the sun had dried the sweat from his curls, making them wild. "I heard one of the cops say there was a scalp on the post. Someone got scalped!"

"Mm hmm." I tuned him out as I wondered how I could find out what Les Pastner, my other suspect, had been up to last night. It wouldn't be easy. The man pretty much kept to himself, living in the woods in a two-room house he had built for himself. It was basically a glorified cabin, and except for his mangy dog, he was alone out there. He had occasionally visited the library to check out books on tracking, the French Revolution, and bombs, but we had never conversed in depth. I had witnessed him once or twice on a good rant at Bonnie and Clyde's, one of two bars in Clitherall, so I knew that he would talk if the right buttons were pressed. I needed to figure out what those buttons were.

Jed interrupted my thoughts. "You hear what everyone is saying? People think the ghost of Wenonga's come back to get us all." He laughed and grabbed another Jolly Rancher. Grape. "Hey, Mir. Wanna have supper tonight? Say, the Rusty Nail at 6:00. I was supposed to meet up with some people to go to the street dance later, but you could hang out with us."

"Sure, Jed. Whatever." I quickly scanned the crowd to make sure Les wasn't here, searching for his telltale greasy gray hair and fatigues, but there were too many people around and I wasn't tall enough to see over most of the heads.

"Great! I'll pick you up."

"What?"

"For supper and the dance tonight. I'll pick you up at 6:00."

Shit. I replayed our conversation in my head. Shit. "No, sorry, I'll meet you at the Nail. I have other plans later."

He looked slightly dejected, or maybe it was just the exertion of our sprint up the block and two Jolly Ranchers catching up with him. "Cool. Some other time."

"Cool." I smiled at Jed, who really was a harmless sort, and pulled out of the crowd. As I walked away, I puzzled over who this Brando person that Kennie had referred to was, and why he would care about the missing Chief. Although it was against my better judgment and actually my survival instinct and every fiber of my being, I decided to go to the source to find out more.

She was not hard to find.

"Kennie?" I said, when I was within speaking distance.

She looked down her nose at me, a few inches taller even in her star spangled ballet slippers. "Hello, Mira. It looks like we'all got ourselves another mystery. Are you on the case?"

"It's pure coincidence that I'm here, though I'd sure like to get the Chief back in time for the Wenonga Days kickoff tonight. Was that Brando person you were talking about part of the entertainment?"

For a second, I thought she was going to ignore me. She probably still felt slighted for being booted from the secured area. Then, in her haughtiest voice, she straightened her red, white, and blue hat and said, "Brando Erikkson is an artist. He and his company, Fibertastic Enterprises, created the Chief." Her voice was raising, and the spangles on her dress started shivering like pebbles before an earthquake. "Do ya' hear me? And we have lost him! WE have LOST him!"

Kennie was working herself into a lather, and lord knows where that would have gone if Mrs. Berns hadn't walked by just then in her flower-patterned housedress and muttered, "You look like ten pounds of shit in a five-pound bag, Rogers."

Immediately, Kennie was back to her plasticine self. "And a good day to you all, too, Mrs. Berns. I can count on you'all helping with the Fourth of July parade cleanup, right?"

Mrs. Berns snorted and kept walking. "I'd rather clean my bathroom with my tongue."

And with that, she was swallowed up by the crowd. I decided to copy her disappearing act and slunk away after a quick "thank you" to Kennie. If I jogged across town, I could maybe track Les down before he opened his store and ask him a few questions in private. That weird little militia guy might be the only thing between me and some uncomfortably long jail time, and that was not a reassuring thought.

Despite its grand name, the Meat and RV Store was just an unassuming brown building off of County Road 210. If not for the enormous red-lettered sign featuring a madly grinning sausage driving a Winnebago, it would have been easy to miss. My Toyota was dwarfed by the five used RVs in the parking lot, every one of which had seen better days. A quick scan of the front of the building revealed no light or movement inside, and when I jogged around back, there was no sign of Les' battered Ford pickup. A quick pull at the rear door revealed that he hadn't arrived.

Unfortunately, there was nothing to do but go back to the library. Maybe I could catch Les on my lunch break. I could almost hear the clock ticking as I drove to work, me racing against the fingerprinting crew. Time was not on my side.

I was a half an hour early opening the library, and Mrs. Berns was a half an hour late. She showed up with a group of elderly friends who were all tittering about the missing statue, the Fourth of July parade, and Kennie's surprise guest. The smell of pressed powder and mint Maalox hovered over them like a cloud.

"I hear Marlon Brando is coming to town!" Ida said. She was one of my favorite old ladies in the world, and Battle Lake had a pretty nice selection. She always looked snappy, and today was no exception. Her hair was a crisp white, cut short, and still in the shape of the curlers that she had slept in. She wore a wrinkle-free yellow polo shirt with the collar neatly ironed, brown shorts with a crease in the front, and brown bobby socks with her white Keds.

"Naw, it's Bronson Pinchot," Mrs. Berns said. I hadn't noticed her flip-flops back at Halvorson Park, but her pink toenails complemented the flowers on her housedress nicely.

"The guy from 'Perfect Strangers'?" Ida asked.

"You sure it's not Charles Bronson coming to town? I heard Charles Bronson." This from Ida's shy sister, Freda. She was dressed almost identical to her sister, except the colors and creases weren't as crisp.

I shook my head. This was how rumors started in small towns. I set Mrs. Berns to the task of reshelving the returned books, waved at her coterie as it old-lady-shuffled out of the building, and got to work on a rough of my "Mira's Musings" column. Given the recent happenings, I decided to title it "It's My Party, and I'll Fly if I Want To":

In a strange turn of events, the Chief Wenonga statue disappeared from Battle Lake just as the plans for his twenty-fifth birthday party were getting under way. Police on the scene Friday morning found only four posts and what appeared

to be blood at the Halvorson Park location where the Chief
has stood proudly for twenty-five years.

The police currently have no leads, and I for sure didn't
do it.

The town of Battle Lake is hoping to have the Chief
home for his holiday. If you have any idea what happened
to the Chief, please email me at miraj@prtel.com.

I crossed out the middle line and chewed on the end of a pen.
My deadline was technically noon Monday, but I wanted to do
more than just write my one column. I wanted to cover all of Wenonga Days, now that it might be Wenonga-less and my ass might
be grass. I phoned Ron Sims to get the go-ahead.

"Hi, Ron. How's tricks?"

Ron was a paunchy, grouchy, warm-hearted man who was for-
tified in life by his dedication to journalism and drive to publicly
make out with his wife. I didn't know if the latter was a fetish so
much as a habit at this point, but if you got Ron and Lisa together,
they sprayed each other like cats in heat. Their dedication was both
heartwarming and stomach turning.

"You got my article, James?"

"Absolutely. Just typed it up. I have a scoop, though."

"Scoop this. Chief Wenonga has disappeared, and we have half
the state coming for his party today."

"I know. I might have an idea where he's gone. I want to cover
the whole weekend. I want to be your Wenonga Days go-to gal," I
said.

"You got until noon Monday to get me 1,500 words. I want at
least three different articles."

"Thanks, Ron!"

"Yup." Click.

I was just about to call Mrs. Berns over to tell her to watch the front while I went to the bathroom when I spotted Battle Lake Police Chief Gary Wohnt striding toward the front glass doors of the library, his shiny lips and fathomless sunglasses reflecting light as sharp as arrows.

SIX

I FELT LIKE CRYING. Could they have matched my fingerprints so quickly? My short life of freedom flashed through my brain. I imagined myself in my garden, soaking up the sun; playing fetch with Luna and being ignored by Tiger Pop; swimming in the cool waters of Whiskey Lake out my front door; eating recognizable food and not showering with strangers. That settled it. I couldn't go to jail. I dropped to the ground and wedged my body into one of the larger open-faced cupboards that made up the tall front counter of the library. Wohnt would need to pass through the "Employees Only" gate at the far side to find me, and I was gambling that he wouldn't do that.

The door donged open, followed by a rapping on the desk above me, two quick knocks, then Wohnt's voice. "Who's on duty?"

When I ducked, the library had been empty except for Mrs. Berns.

"Hello?" Wohnt's voice was impatient. I heard him step away from the desk and walk to the far wall, near the turning racks that housed the fiction paperbacks, then return to the front, moving closer to the gate that would admit him behind the counter. "Anyone?"

From where I was shaking, I could see his hands curl round the swinging gate. Not only had he discovered my fingerprints on Chief Wenonga's post, he was also about to find me hiding in a cupboard in the library. Not good. I tried to scrounge up a solid lie, but my brain was numb. I was going to jail.

"They don't teach you how to read in cop school? That there gate says 'Employees Only.'"

Mrs. Berns' voice stopped Wohnt in mid-opening position, and he let the gate swing back. She brushed past him and stood on the other side of the opening, arms crossed. Relief left me lightheaded.

"Where's Mira James?"

"Probably chasing after that Johnny Leeson, if she's got any brains."

Jeez. Did everyone know?

"She's not working?"

"Not today. I've been promoted to vice president of the library, and today is my first day in charge. Need a book? Oh!" Mrs. Berns pursed her lips dramatically. "That's right. You can't read." She shook her head sadly.

Wohnt's fist came down once, hard, on the countertop, and I heard him suck in a deep breath. When he spoke, his words came out slowly. "When you see Ms. James, tell her I need to speak with her. Immediately, if not sooner."

"Over and out."

I didn't move, even after I heard the front door open angrily and then swing shut.

Mrs. Berns kept her eyes forward. "Vice president. That means I probably need a raise."

"Deal," I said.

"Deal. Say, did you hear Charles Bronson is coming to town for the Fourth of July parade? I'm so excited!" She went back to her reshelving, and I crawled out of the cupboard, still shaky. Not only did I need to find a twenty-three-foot tall fiberglass statue and a semi-scalped man, I had to accomplish this while avoiding Gary Wohnt and his posse. I snuck out of work during my lunch break, leaving the new vice president to handle the clientele and to lock up. I took a risk in driving my car home, but my future freedom depended on getting to the bottom of all this as quickly as possible.

There was no SWAT team at the double-wide, just Luna and Tiger Pop greeting me with love and warm indifference, respectively. I rushed in and got all three of us fresh food and water— kibbles for the dog and cat, an American cheese and sliced pickle sandwich on wheat for me. After our tummies were full, I took Luna for a walk and Tiger Pop for a follow down to the beach at the end of my driveway. Luna romped in the water, enjoying the cooling droplets in her fur. While Luna swam, I scoured the woods for wild catnip for Tiger Pop and found a bumper crop. After Luna had cooled off, the three of us moseyed back to the house, where I did some dusting, vacuuming, and bathroom scrubbing, and they cheered me on, silently, from a cool spot on the kitchen linoleum.

When suppertime neared, I pulled my hair up under a baseball cap and changed into touristy clothing—a pair of white shorts I found in Sunny's storage room and a pastel-blue blouse I had bought for my last job interview. Battle Lake is a small town, but it sees a lot of summer traffic, particularly around the Fourth and Wenonga Days. If I rode Sunny's bike the three miles to town and kept my hat on, I could blend right in.

If I took the tar, I'd have lots of hills but some shade. The gravel road to town meandered through fields and so was flatter but tree-free. I hopped on my bike, the muggy air licking at me like a devil's tongue, and opted for the tar. My bike only had three gears, but I managed to make it all the way to town without having to get off and walk up any hills. I was proud, but sweaty.

Thankfully, Battle Lake was hopping. Granny's Pantry on Lake Street was open, and the lawn chairs out front were full of sticky kids eating ice cream cones bigger than their heads. Down the street, Ace Hardware was featuring a Fourth of July Weekend Special, which meant that they would stay open until nine. A row of shiny Weber grills lined the sidewalk to tantalize the tourist crowd. Farther up the street, Stub's Dinner Club, which looked like an enormous blue pole barn any way you sliced it, was packed to overflowing. Patrons were parking in Larry's Grocery parking lot across the road to get in line to wait for one of Stub's famous butter knife steaks with a side of Lyonnaise hashbrowns.

Carefree summer chatter filled the air, and every third truck on the main drag was pulling a boat. As I biked past the Dairy Queen, sniffing in the smell of roasting meat, I heard snatches of a light-hearted squabble over whether leeches or swamp frogs worked best for catching walleye. I kept my head down, confident that I was not conspicuous.

The Rusty Nail had a choice corner location in downtown Battle Lake, and its log cabin exterior was welcoming. I was relieved that the place was packed so I could blend into the crowd. I was batting whatever is a really good number to bat.

The Nail was full of beer air and people out early in anticipation of the street dance, which was customarily held on the paved street right outside its front door. The band Kennie had found for tonight was called "Not with My Horse." She swore they covered country and rock favorites and would be real crowd pleasers. I didn't listen to much country, and I wasn't looking forward to hearing "You Shook Me All Night Long" for the quadrillionth time, but the horde would provide great cover later as I sought out information on the missing Chief.

I found a table in the back, poorly lit poolroom and waited for Jed. I knew the police would be busy on the road and handling crowd control tonight, but I didn't want to take any chances, so I kept my back to the door.

"Mir? That you? What're you, in-cog-neeee-to?" Jed was wearing a dark blue bandana tied over his curly hair like a helmet, a faded Rolling Stones T-shirt with a gigantic red tongue on the front, and faded Levis out of which poked hobbit-haired toes in flip-flops.

I glanced quickly over at Jed. "Shh! Sit down."

"What's up with you? You're all nervous and weird."

"It's this Chief Wenonga stuff. You heard anything?"

"Them cops don't know nothin', and no one's seen the Chief." He whooped, and slapped his knee. "Wohnt is pretty pissed that

Wenonga is missing. Makes him look like an idiot! He's running around town kickin' butt and taking names."

I set down the menu I had been holding. I didn't feel so hungry anymore. Jed continued, oblivious to my discomfort.

"I stayed and watched them scrape that piece of head off the post. I suppose they'll know something about that soon enough, but I don't know what they're expecting to find. They'd be better off looking for a guy with a hat!"

"What?"

"A guy with a hat. Cuz' he's missing a piece of his head?" Jed smiled at me.

Suddenly, the air in the Nail became greasy and close. "That's a rich one, Jed. Um, I'm not feeling so good. Can I take a rain check on supper?"

Jed's face fell. "Sure. No problem. How about tomorrow, same time, same place?"

"I'll call you, 'kay?" I ducked outside with my head down and veered into the alley running behind the Nail to inhale some fresh air. There were spindly elms growing around the Dumpster, and from the rear of the building, I saw that the logs on the front were just cheap siding. On the alley side, the building was crumbling brick.

I lodged myself in a dark nook, upwind from the garbage, and collected my thoughts. Wohnt was after me because my fingerprints were found next to a bloody scalp. I had no alibi for last night, and my behavior had been suspicious, pretty much since I'd moved to Battle Lake. I was formulating a plan to clear my name when a voice cut through my thoughts. "Now, this was the last place I expected to find you."

SEVEN

I SQUEAKED AND JUMPED back, scraping my elbow on the brick.

The melodic voice laughed. "Sorry, Mira. I didn't mean to scare you. But what do you expect when you're hiding in the alley behind a bar?"

I rubbed the raw spot on my elbow and glared at Dr. Castle. Had she intentionally scared me? Her eyes were guileless, and she smiled warmly at me, her mouth as wide as the Cheshire cat's. I relaxed half a notch.

"I'm not hiding." I squinted up and down the alley to make sure no one else was sneaking up on me. A laughing couple in clicky cowboy boots strolled past on the street, but otherwise, I couldn't see anyone. "I came out here to get away from the cigarette smoke. What are *you* doing in the alley?"

"Looking for you. I stopped by early for a bite, and your friend told me you had just left. If the smoke bothers you, we could go somewhere else."

The abrasion on my elbow made me crabby, and I wanted to just come out and ask her if she had stolen the Chief, but she didn't know me and I didn't know her. "How about the Fortune Café? They have a deck off the back."

"Perfect! I've been meaning to check that place out since I got to town. Mind if we walk?"

"Not at all."

If she wondered why I kept to the unlit back streets, she didn't ask. When we reached the Fortune, I sent the doctor to the deck and pulled Sid aside. I explained that I was avoiding Wohnt, and she didn't ask questions. I brought out herbal iced tea and sugar cookies and sat down next to Dr. Castle.

For the first time, I noticed what a gorgeous night it was going to be. The sun had two hours left on the horizon, and it was reflecting pinks and dusty purples off the treetops, the intense heat of the day making the colors more vivid than usual. The air smelled like water and woodsmoke, and I could hear the pop of firecrackers and a family laughing in their backyard. The pleasant sounds would be drowned out in exactly one hour by the twang of raucous country guitars, but for right now, the town was beautiful. I forced myself to relax. I needed Dr. Castle to be able to feel comfortable enough to confide in me.

"How do you like Battle Lake so far, Dr. Castle?" I was actually a little intimidated by her, now that we were one-on-one. As recently as last winter, I had been a professional college student, and although I was the same age as her, she seemed more confident and much smarter.

"Dolly. You can call me Dolly, and I like the town just fine. The people seem very warm."

"Really?" I didn't hide my surprise well.

"Really. What, you thought they'd be mean to me because I'm taking away the Chief?"

"You mean, you *were* taking the Chief, until he disappeared."

"Funny timing, that." Her eyes were hooded, and I couldn't tell if she was relaxed or hiding.

"Mmm-hmm. So since he's gone, your work here is done?"

"Oh no. Chief Wenonga was the symbol of the sort of thing PEAS is fighting, but he wasn't ever the only problem. I'm hoping to do away with the festival entirely."

I stirred sugar into my icy tea and played devil's advocate, hoping to mine some information. "Is the festival so bad? People don't even really know what they're celebrating. They just want an excuse to get together and have some fun." It was a plausible argument. In Otter Tail County, where we outshone the country in per capita sales of fishing licenses, we had 1.004 men for every woman, the median age was 41.1, and the mean temperature was not much higher, people deserved distractions.

"Ignorance is not an excuse, am I right?" The question came out gently, but I noticed her neck tense. "Objects sacred to the First Nations are used as tourist attractions, and that's offensive to those who respect spirituality. Stereotypical representations of Native American men, like the Chief Wenonga statue, limit the role and history of Native American men to that of violent warriors. They also ignore modern cultural experiences of native people and the roles of women and children. Is that necessary?"

"I never thought about all that. Maybe we should appease Les and put up a drunken Irishman statue." I laughed, hoping my lame joke would get a reaction from her, but she sat still but for her breathing, studying me. I changed the subject. "You know they found fingerprints at the base of the Chief, right? It won't be long until they match those with the culprit."

Still no movement. "The culprit would have to have their fingerprints in the system, wouldn't they?"

I blinked once, then again. Of course! If a person has never committed a crime, they wouldn't ever be fingerprinted. If they'd never been fingerprinted, there would be no way to match them to a crime unless they were a suspect. I laughed with joy. I had never been fingerprinted in my life. As long as no one saw me at Halvorson Park this morning, or could trace the 911 call to me, I was safe. I just had to stay under Wohnt's radar until I found the thief, who was possibly a murderer.

I grinned at Dolly Castle, who appeared to be laughing silently at me. "You look mightily relieved," she said, "as if you just got a pardon. Maybe you have something you want to share?"

For a second, I thought we could be friends, but not until I was permanently off the hook and someone else was on. And that someone might still turn out to be Dolly.

I backed off my smile. "How're the cookies?"

Dolly's eyes, which she directed over my shoulder and at the door to the main café, widened. "They just got considerably better."

I craned my neck, keeping the bill of my cap down, to see what had put the purr in her. My gray eyes connected squarely with Johnny Leeson's deep blues.

EIGHT

Somehow in the previous week I had forgotten how beautiful Johnny was, with his shaggy, dark blonde hair, thick eyelashes, and soft, gently smiling mouth. His hands were strong and tanned, the kind of hands that you wanted moving slowly down your naked back and tangled in your hair as he pulled you in for a deep kiss. His broad shoulders tapered nicely to narrow hips, and it took all my willpower not to imagine what it would be like to have my legs wrapped around them. I crossed said legs to muffle the excited whispering down below and gave him a short nod. Men had always been bad news for me, in a cheating and dying sort of way, and I had vowed to start listening to my brain more and my nerve endings less. It was high time I focused my energy on a more reliable form of entertainment. Like tornado chasing. I drew in a deep breath and concentrated on slowing down my heartbeat, which had revved at the sight of Johnny.

I wasn't surprised to see Jed follow Johnny out onto the Fortune deck. The two were the local odd jobs, taking on landscaping and heavy lifting work on the side, and they often hung out in their off hours as well. I hoped Jed wouldn't feel bad to see that I was still out. Johnny waved at me with one of his gorgeous hands and started to pull up a chair at a far table, but Jed loped over.

"Hey, Mira! You must be feeling better. And you know what I forgot to ask you? Now that someone stole the Chief, who you gonna crush on?" Jed smiled and slapped his knee.

Was my pitiful, make-believe love life written on my forehead? Or more likely, a billboard on the edge of town? "Good one." I tried to send out "go away" vibes because I didn't want Johnny to notice that I was dressed like a dorky tourist, and I especially didn't want him to hear that I thought Chief Wenonga was hot. If finding out that you like really big fiberglass men doesn't turn a guy off you, then you don't want him.

Jed, as always, was oblivious to social cues. "You guys got two extra chairs. Awesome!" He signaled to Johnny.

He walked over and flashed his killer shy smile at me. "Hi, Mira. How're you doing?"

"Fine."

"Mind if we sit here?"

"Not at all," Dolly said, indicating the chair nearest her. "I don't believe we've met."

I thought I detected a faint burning smell. It might have been the sizzling Dolly was directing at Johnny, or possibly my hopes of being the object of his unrequited love going up in smoke. I had no choice but to make the introductions. "This is Johnny Lee-son. He works at the greenhouse here in town. And this is Jed." Jed smiled and nodded through a mouthful of our sugar cookies, but the doctor didn't bother to look his way.

"A horticulturalist? That's so fascinating! Where'd you study?" Dolly's smile was ear to ear, and she was leaning in to hear Johnny's response.

He pulled back a little, or maybe it was just wishful thinking on my part. "U of M. I'm going to grab a couple sodas. Can I get you two anything?"

"Soda?" Dolly asked. "You must have spent some time in Wisconsin. No one in Minnesota calls it 'soda.'"

"Yeah, my grandparents are from Wausau. I spent a lot of summers at their place. So you two are fine?"

"Yeah, we're fine. Thanks," I said. When Johnny stood up, I caught a whiff of him. He smelled clean and solid, like a cherry Popsicle stick. I forced myself not to look at his firm-like-a-new-mattress rear as he walked away. If I had a pair of x-ray goggles, my willpower might not have been so strong.

"Hey, you're the Indian doctor, aren't you?" Jed asked.

"Close. I'm a professor of Native American Studies. What do you do?"

"I work at my parents' resort. It's a pretty good job, but…oh, shit!"

Before you could say "smoke," Jed leapt up and over the railing of the Fortune Café deck with surprising agility. I glanced behind me to see what had made him scurry, and was alarmed to make out the rear bumper of a black and white pulling up in front of the café. At this angle, the police inside the vehicle wouldn't be able to see who was in back, especially in the dusky light. I was pretty sure that Gary Wohnt didn't have anything on me, but I didn't like the way he kept turning up. Maybe somebody had seen me at Halvorson Park, after all. I looked at Jed's retreating figure, then at the door Johnny had just left through. Would I rather risk going to jail, or leave Dolly alone to flirt with Johnny? Cripes. It's tough being single. I dropped a couple dollars on the table for a tip and jumped over the rail.

"I better go see what's up with Jed," I said. "Tell Johnny bye from me."

Dolly smiled, but didn't respond. I made my way through the back alleys until I reached my bike parked out of the streetlights' glare near the Rusty Nail. I had never intended to follow Jed, who probably at this very moment was burying a roach and some Zig-Zags in someone's backyard. I just needed to get away from the police. Since I was on the move, I decided to swing past the Meat and RV Store, the simmering air brushing past me as I pedaled, washing thoughts of Johnny out of my head. For now.

Les' store was on the south side of town, facing 210, about five blocks from the Fortune Café. When I reached it, I was happily surprised to see a light still on. It was dim, filtering from the back room through the glass panel of the front, but it gave me hope that there would be someone here. I leaned my bike against the building and crunched up to the front window. The "closed" sign was face out, but I could see shadows playing against the light of the back room.

I strode to the rear of the building just as the back door slammed open. I retreated into the shadows out of instinct and was only able to catch a sideways glimpse of the person leaving. He was over six feet tall, with dark hair pulled back in a pony tail. His nose was sharp and arrogant, and his lips were tight in concentration. He strode toward a blood-red Humvee I hadn't noticed parked behind a Winnebago that was up on blocks. An image abruptly sewed itself into my mind—it was a picture of a red Humvee in my rearview mirror. Not many of those around, even in the summer. Could this guy be the same person I had seen driving toward Chief Wenonga's post this morning? I'd take that bet.

I heard the "beep beep" of a security system unlocking the Hummer doors, which was a funny sound in Battle Lake. No one here locked their houses, let alone their cars.

Before tall, dark, and angry escaped, Les flung himself out of the back door. He wore a Cenex cap that was too big for his head and threatening to tip off. "Wait!"

The stranger turned around. "I don't think so."

"But it's a good idea!" Les was jogging toward the Humvee, which rumbled awake and carried its mysterious passenger away. Les just stood and watched it go, delicately adjusting his hat.

"Les?"

He jumped at my voice. "Who's there?"

"It's me, Mira. From the library? How're you?"

"Don't ask." Les kicked past me, a tight ball of anger in his camouflage T-shirt and pants. He didn't look at me as he reentered his shop and slammed the back door shut. I heard the click of a lock on the other side.

"Les? Mr. Pastner? I just want to ask you a couple questions about the Chief Wenonga statue. Mr. Pastner?" I drummed on the back door for a minute or two before I gave up. If there's anything a militia guy is good at, it's waiting.

From the direction of town, I heard the muffled chords of an electric guitar warming up, signaling the beginning of the street dance. I could either go home and avoid Wohnt, or I could go to the dance and try to hook up with Dolly again. I would risk possible jail time, and worse, I would risk Johnny seeing me again in these horrible clothes, but I was never one to hide, at least not since I'd been on my own. Life had taught me that a moving target is harder to hit.

I walked my bike the five blocks back to the street dance, weaving around the cars scrabbling for a parking spot and pedestrians laughing and drinking beer out of plastic cups. The mood was festive, and it was early enough that there were still kids out, excited to be among the grownups at night. I couldn't squeeze my bike past the throng outside the Rusty Nail, so I walked it across to Larry's parking lot and hid it behind a row of yellow-blooming potentilla shrubs, careful to avoid the streetlights.

The closer I drew to the street dance, the more heinous the music became. Fortunately, pretty much any music will do if you're outside on a hot summer night with a cold beer, and the crowds I passed seemed to be either ignoring the music or laughing at it. I decided to walk the perimeter of the street dance and come around behind it, where it would be quieter. I didn't spot Dolly Castle or Johnny anywhere I looked. I suppose they could still be on the deck at the Fortune, but I didn't have the heart to check.

As I ducked into the alley one block up from the band, I caught a glimpse of two flashing balls. I realized they were electric earrings, and a second later, saw they were attached to Kennie. I slid behind an oak tree and peeked out at her, about forty feet from me. We were on the edge of the residential part of Battle Lake, right where the businesses ended and homes started. She was talking to the man I had seen drive off in the red Humvee, and they were walking toward me. Their conversation drifted over the music.

"...so embarrassed the Chief has gone missing."

"Don't worry, Kennie. We'll make it work."

Kennie caressed his arm and giggled into his eyes. I was put off by her sloppy flirting. Even though Kennie and Gary Wohnt went to great pains to hide their relationship, the whole town knew they were dating, and her current lite infidelity did not sit well with me. "I know we will, Brando. I know we will."

Brando. Brando Erikkson, the owner of the company that had created Chief Wenonga. He was walking like a man proud of his hair shirt, tall and strong, swinging his glossy black hair in the night and cutting his eyes at Kennie. What had the owner of an out-of-town fiberglass company been doing at Les' Meat and RV?

Suddenly, the silence was deafening. The band was taking a break, and Kennie and Brando were almost on top of me. I slid around the tree inch by inch as they neared, staying just out of their sight. I waited for the count of twenty, listening to their footfalls grow fainter. Then I scooted out to follow them, my eyes darting side to side, which is exactly why I didn't notice the solid, six-feet-two-inch mass in front of me until I railroaded right into it.

My eyes slowly traveled up the unyielding, muscular body to the face, my heart thudding. Had I misjudged? Had Brando backtracked to catch me? When my reluctant eyes met the gaze of the man in front of me, I froze. Oh, this was much worse than Brando. Much worse than anything I could have dreamed up in my worst nightmare, as a matter of fact.

NINE

To my horror, I was looking into the blank eyes of Bad Brad. He and I had been dating when I left the Twin Cities in March, and the last time I had seen him, his eyeballs had been closed in bliss as the hussy dog-sitting for my neighbor played his skin flute, accompanied by the hard-to-find CD of Portuguese woodwinds that I had recently purchased for him. He didn't know that I had caught them in the act, as I had been perched on the second-story roof of a West Bank apartment spying down at him from a skylight. Shortly after I witnessed Brad Cheater Pants in the act, he got into a mysterious bike accident. Seems the nuts holding his front tire to the rest of his bike had disappeared. I felt bad, for a minute. Then, I broke up with him and moved away, never telling him why we were through. It hadn't seemed particularly important that he know. Or, was it that I didn't like confrontations?

"Mira?" He grabbed my shoulder and held me arm's length away. "Did you come to see my show?"

Brad was still cute, in his blonde Jim Morrison sort of way. And still dumb as a turd. "Hi, Brad. No, I live here now."

"In Battle Creek?"

"Battle Lake."

"Yeah. You hear me play? This new band is tight!" He brushed his curling hair back and looked at me with his clear blue eyes, smiling eagerly.

"I thought Not with My Horse was going to be a country band."

"Oh, we are! But with our own style, you know? That last song? It was 'My Achey Breaky Heart Belongs to Satan.' Fuckin' cool shit."

I looked at my feet and shook my head. This man had seen me naked. I had made breakfast in bed for this man. I had even listened to his poetry and told him it was luminous. Running into exes is its own special brand of hell because it reminds you what a dumbass you used to be. All I can say is that even monkeys learn from their mistakes. "Well, it was nice seeing you again. You take care."

"Not so fast! Why don't you hear our next set? There's a song about you in there."

I stopped on my heel and turned back. "Really?"

"Yup."

"What's it called?"

"Mira Mira." Brad dropped to one knee and clutched my hand, belting out a tune in a wailing country twang: "Mira, Mira, on my wall, tell me who is the rockingest fool of all, no wait a minute, I think I see, the answer staring back at me." Brad rose, swiveled his hips and raised his voice. Out of the corner of my mortified eyes,

I could see a crowd beginning to gather. "Oooh! Mira, Mira on the wall, spent most of my life lying in bed, breakfast was vodka-soaked bread and a pack of cigarettes. Yow! Mira, Mira, they say it'll kill me, but I got a feeling, if I head next door for some loving, I'll start healing."

I glanced around at the handful of people swaying to Brad's painful serenade and wondered how long it would take to chew off my hand so I could escape into the night. That's when I spotted Johnny and Dolly strolling toward me, her arm looped in his. My heart dropped from my chest into my stomach and rolled around a little in the gastric juices, like a side of meat getting beer battered. Johnny and Dr. Dolly. It was bad enough they were together, but I'd be damned if I'd let them see me being howled to by this mistake.

I flicked Brad in the nose like a bad dog, and when he released my hand, took off jogging. I hopped on my bike and kept to the back streets until I got to County Road 83, which I hung to for about half a mile before I turned right onto the gravel. When I arrived home, I was too wired and disappointed—no closer to finding the Chief, had lost Johnny to a better woman, and one big bad ex was in town—to sleep. I decided to hit the garden.

It had been a fertile year, with unusually hot weather. My tangled backyard was dense as a jungle, and the apple trees on the perimeter were thick with sour, baby-fist-sized fruit. I changed into faded cut-offs and a tank top, the night air still a moist 96 degrees according to the yardlight-lit, sun-shaped thermometer hanging outside my front door. I could smell the heavy sugar-scent of roses blooming around the side of the house, and underneath that trailed the scent of woodsmoke. Somebody must be having a bonfire. The smell of wood burning on a warm summer night spells comfort for a Minnesota girl. It's in our genes. I resolved to force thoughts of Brad and Johnny out of my mind. Back into the junk drawer for those two.

I gardened by moon- and yard-light, starting in on the east side of the garden with the row of marigolds. They were golden and spicy, and their thick furry leaves cast too much shade to allow many weeds to take root below. That row was clean in under ten minutes. Next, I hoed the wide space between my twelve staked tomato plants. These were flowering like mad, and before I weeded the base I snipped the small leaves in the fork of the branches so the plants would have more vigor to bear fruit. The snipped baby leaves left a wet, peppery streak on my fingers. Once the tomatoes were weeded, the earth around them as clean and warm as a brown blanket, I moved on to the onions, planting one foot on each side of the row as I gently dug out the pigweed growing around the bulbs.

Tiger Pop and Luna stretched themselves out on the still-warm black dirt at the edge of the garden and ignored me as best they could. By the time I finished the onions and swung over to the row of coffee can–clad broccoli, cauliflower, and Brussels sprouts, the bugs were as thick as soup. They had found me, and it was time to quit. Not for the first time, I wished mosquitoes had radiant butts like fireflies so they could at least light the way as they drilled into skin. If they had the power to glow, tonight would be lit up like the northern lights.

Swatting at the buzzing horde, I dashed for the double-wide, my hard-earned respite gone. Tomorrow was the Fourth of July, and I needed to evade the police, find a man missing part of his head, and track down a twenty-three-foot statue. While I was juggling that fun to-do list, I also needed to cover the fireworks display for the *Battle Lake Recall,* avoid a cheating ex-boyfriend who may or may not be spending the weekend in town, and convince myself that I hadn't really been falling for Johnny. The only silver lining was that the library would be closed for the holiday, so I'd have time to nose around.

The first person on tomorrow's To-Snoop list was definitely shifty Les Pastner. He had evaded me twice, first by not being at the Meat and RV this morning and second by locking the door on me tonight. I scratched at a mosquito bite behind my ear and thought about maybe wearing a hat next time I weeded at night to deter the bugs from my more tender areas. That's when I remembered Les' hat, perched tenderly on his head as he chased after the mysterious man with the Humvee, who had turned out to be Brando Erikkson. I had never thought of Les as a hat person.

Click.

Of course. Jed had said the police should look for a person wearing a hat because he'd be missing part of his scalp. Les had been wearing a big, loose cap the last time I had seen him, and he had been acting awfully suspiciously since the fake Wenonga Days planning meeting. If I couldn't force Les to talk to me, at least I could peek under his hat.

TEN

THE FOURTH OF JULY dawned hot and bright. The air was thick, and out my front windows the sun sparkled off the serene surface of Whiskey Lake. It was going to be another breeze-free scorcher. I stood under an ice cold shower, wrapped my hair in a bun off my neck, and donned a cotton baby doll sundress that let the air flow freely on my back and legs. Before I poured fresh water for Luna and Tiger Pop, I packed their bowls with ice cubes so their water wouldn't boil while I was gone. I even retrieved two oranges from the crisper drawer of the fridge, sliced them in half, and nailed them to the birdhouse in the shade of the large oak tree in my yard so the orioles could chill a little. Birds and I didn't get along, and since they had the aerial advantage, I went out of my way to be nice to them. They were the avian equivalents of playground bullies, as far as I was concerned.

My bird aversion probably had something to do with misplaced guilt. When I was four and a half, my cousin Heather and I found a robin's nest in our climbing tree. There were three newly hatched babies inside, their featherless skin translucent. Heather warned me not to touch them because then their mom wouldn't come back. I pretended to listen to her, but deep inside, I knew that I was meant to take care of one of those robins. It would grow up believing I was its mom, and it would sing on my shoulder just like in a Disney movie. We would be tight.

Later, when I was supposed to be napping, I returned to the nest and snatched the weak little thing, I concealed it in the very back of my sock drawer, which was little-used in the summer. I also pilfered a pound of raw hamburger from the pile in the freezer and set it next to the baby. My attention span being what it was, I quickly forgot both baby and burger until the smell became thick like air vomit. I found the bird, five days after I placed it in there, tiny eyes closed forever behind see-through lids. The hamburger was greenish and flirting with maggots. I tossed the burger in the woods and buried the bird in a shallow grave next to my Barbie doll whose head I had accidentally popped off.

I knew I was the reason the baby bird had died, and if I had only listened to my cousin, it would still be alive and maybe raising some babies of its own. Since that day, I figured the birds knew me for what I was, and I avoided them at all costs. I pretended it was because I didn't like them, but the truth was, they had every reason not to like me. I was always on guard for the retributive poop missiles, and this sizzling day would be no exception.

My community ed class with Johnny Leeson was scheduled for 10:00, with the Wenonga Days parade right on its heels at eleven, followed by some Les-hunting at noon. That plan of attack allowed me enough time to wash some clothes, compose a shopping list, and write a postcard to my friend Sunny, whose house I was sitting. As far as I knew, she was still on a fishing boat in Alaska with her mono-browed lover, Rodney, but she had given me the address of the company's central office, so I had some place to send mail to. I mulled over what to tell her about the current Wenonga situation. I didn't like to lie, at least to my friends, but I didn't want her to accuse me of keeping anything from her should all this have a bad ending. I needed to word it just so:

Hey, Sunshine! It is so frickin' hot in Battle Lake that my freckles have melted. Luna is doing fine, though I think she might be getting a little pudgy—I'm going to start taking her on more walks. As Chief Wenonga Days approaches, I can't help but notice something is missing. Isn't this the first time in your life you haven't been at a Wenonga Days parade? Big love! Mira

I was covered. Hopefully, by the time Sunny phoned, which she did every two weeks or so, this would all be solved, the Chief would be back in place, and I'd only have good news to report. I washed, dried, folded, and put away two loads of clothes, realized that I didn't need anything from the grocery store besides bagels, cream cheese, and orange juice, and let the animals outside with their ice water placed in the shade. I slid gingerly into my dragon's mouth of a car. I tuned my radio to the rock station out of Fergus Falls, rolled down the windows, and drove as fast as the gravel would allow to move some air.

It wasn't until I passed a police car on the north side of Battle Lake, parked amid the traffic of the weekend flea market, that I remembered that driving my car wasn't a smart move. On a bike, I could blend in. In my 1982 champagne brown Toyota Corolla hatchback, I was a fish in a barrel. I hunched down into my seat, trying to tighten my ear skin so the anticipated police sirens wouldn't sound so shrieking harsh as Wohnt hunted me down like a dog. When the air stayed blessedly silent, minus the nasal twang of CCR floating out of my radio, I dared a glance in my rearview mirror. The police car was empty, its occupant likely patrolling in the mayhem of the flea market.

Four blocks ahead, another police rig was parked, and I could just make out Gary Wohnt steering cars away from the marked-off parade route. It was too early in the day to be dumb twice, so I lurched a sharp right and purred down the back streets of Battle Lake. If I brought my car home, I'd never make it back in time for the parade, so I pulled up into an alley and left the Toyota in the rear driveway of my friend Gina's house. A quick knock at her door told me she wasn't home, but when I tried her doorknob, it turned. I went inside, grabbed a red, white, and blue Minnesota Twins baseball cap off the rack next to the door, left a quick note, and headed toward the high school where Johnny's gardening class was being held.

In most parts of the United States, community education classes aren't held on national holidays. In Battle Lake, a local ladies' gardening club had started a petition to have Johnny's classes held every Saturday morning, come holidays, hell, or high water. Their reasoning was that he was providing an important service to the community and that many of his students were tourists, who were the thickest on the weekend holidays. This was true and true, if you agreed that looking hot at a chalkboard is an important service and that the out-of-town friends and family of the ladies' gardening club count as tourists.

I had debated not coming to today's class, but then I would have had to admit to myself that I really liked Johnny. Inside the classroom, I slid into the back row, next to two chirpy women in their early twenties. They both had golden hair, and the fluorescent lighting picked up their perfect honey highlights. Their skin was tawny, their breasts impossibly full yet perky, and I bet I couldn't have found an inch of cellulite on them even if I tweaked them head to toe in a vise grip, one inch at a time. I'd attended enough of Johnny's classes to know that they were the young groupies.

They scooched their chairs over slightly as I sat down and whispered between themselves, glancing cattily at me. I was in a suddenly foul mood, so I decided to play with them.

"Hi. I'm Mira."

They both studied me for a beat or two and decided I wasn't competition. "I'm Heaven, and this is Brittany."

I nodded at both of them. I knew the type—fresh out of high school, sure of their place in the world but ultimately lacking confidence in anything other than their immaculate makeup and hairless bodies. If they didn't wise up in the near future, they'd be married and pregnant within two years. Meanwhile, they looked like they had just stepped out of a J. Crew catalog, and it was cheesing me off.

"You guys like to garden?"

This sent them into peals of laughter. Heaven caught her breath first. "No, chick. We don't come for the gardening."

I chafed at the condescension in her voice and was gearing up for a verbal smackdown, but just then Johnny walked in, thick hair spilling around his sun-browned face. He scanned the room, stopping tentatively when he spotted me, and walked to the front of the classroom. My dirt-grimed fingernails from last night's gardening suddenly seemed conspicuous, so I sat on my hands.

"Hello, everyone. Thanks for coming. Today, we're going to talk about the second sowings of beets and lettuce—when to do it, what types of seeds to use, and where and how to plant them. I'm glad you're here, and I want you to know that in this class, there's no such thing as a dumb question."

Heaven raised her hand. "What do you consider a dumb question?"

I rolled my eyes under the bill of the Twins cap. I'd be surprised if this one was smart enough to turn left, yet here she was, pretty pretty pretty and making me feel like a dirt clump next to her.

"Heaven, right? Don't worry about it. Just ask any questions you have." He smiled encouragingly and turned to the chalkboard. His arm muscles, lean from outdoor work, rippled as he made notes.

We all had three tight packages of Seeds of Change organic seeds on our desks—one Detroit Dark Red beet, a depiction of lusciously maroon beets like pirate's jewels amid deep-green leaves on the front of the packet; one Buttercrunch lettuce with a picture of a thick and tender head of greens on its front; and one Emerald Oak Looseleaf lettuce with bright green leaves as delicate and whorled as a baby's ears gracing the packet. I slid off my right hand and shook the Buttercrunch packet, enjoying the grainy sound of the seeds falling all over one another.

Despite my best intentions to remain crabby and distant, I became lost in Johnny's smooth, deep voice as he explained that it was probably best to sow beets every two weeks for the first two thirds of the summer to keep up a regular supply. I was a sucker for earth-friendly guys, and by the end of class, I had almost forgotten that he was no longer mine. When he stopped at the end to take questions, Brittany shot her hand into the air, wafting a fruity dose of Baby Phat perfume my way.

When she caught Johnny's attention, she tossed her golden hair over her shoulder and leaned forward, showing the world her front butt as it spilled out of her tank top.

"Do you prefer to garden with gloves, or without?"

The class listened anxiously, all eighteen women eager to learn what Johnny wore when he gardened.

Johnny answered with his characteristic honesty, oblivious to the adulation he was garnering. "I like to feel the dirt on my hands. I garden bare."

A soft groan swept through his audience.

"Any other questions?"

"Do you give home gardening seminars? Like at someone's house?"

This second question came from Heaven, who was tracing a finger around the edges of her pink-glossed lips.

"Sure. Why don't you stay after class and I can give you more information."

Heaven and Brittany squirmed in their seats at the invite, and that was the end of class. I scooped up my seeds and bolted toward the door.

"Mira? Can you hang on a second?"

Johnny was walking toward me as the rest of the class gathered their belongings and broke off into clumps to say their see ya' laters.

Johnny gently tugged my elbow and guided me toward the hall, and I couldn't remember if he'd ever intentionally touched me before. I was acutely aware of my dirty nails and the beat of my heart. Certain that Johnny was going to ask me why in the hell an industrial jazz rocker had serenaded me last night, I looked everywhere but into his face.

He was silent for a few seconds, then asked quietly, "Is something wrong?"

I shook my head no and kept studying my sandals, my blue-painted toenails peeking out.

"You were really quiet in class today."

I sighed, resigned, and looked up into his disarming, cobalt-blue eyes, trying to keep my voice light and pleasant. "I've got a lot going on. What can I do for you?"

Just then, Heaven walked into the hall. "Can we talk, Johnny?"

"Sure," he said, waving her back into the classroom. "Give me a second." His hand still gripped my elbow, and it felt warm and strong.

When Heaven was out of earshot, he turned back to me. "I want to talk to you, but it might take awhile. Are you free tonight?"

My heart seriously skipped a beat. Was he asking me out on a date? All thoughts of Dolly and self-pity melted away, and with them, my newfound distant-cool attitude around Johnny. "I really like you!"

Johnny gave me a puzzled look. "You really like me?"

"No. I mean, I meant to say that I'd really like *to*…um, do something with you later. If I'm free, you know, but I think I am." I guess a gal never gets too old to be stupid *and* easy.

My sudden wave of uncool still had Johnny thrown. He dropped his hand from my elbow. "Good. Yeah, good. I'll pick you up at 6:00, and we can go out for supper."

I wanted to say something that would linger with him until tonight, but all that came out was, "I love supper!"

Johnny smiled a strange smile at me and walked back into the classroom.

Maybe I had misjudged Johnny and Dolly's hanging out last night. They could have been talking about Wisconsin, for all I knew, since both had spent a lot of time there. I literally skipped to the front door and floated to the *Recall* office to pick up the digital camera before I headed to the Kiddie Karnival. The carnival was always held right off Lake Street in the parking lot of the fire hall. It was actually a pretty lame event, if you knew better. If you were four, though, the fishing for plastic ducks, throwing darts at balloons, and tossing rings on old glass Coke bottles was nirvana, and everyone left a winner with a pocketful of Tootsie Rolls.

The Turtle Races, however, were a little grimmer. The turtles started in the center of the pavement, where there was a four-foot-diameter circle permanently painted. The first turtle to make it outside the circle won. The pavement at the First National Bank parking lot had been sprayed with hoses, but it seemed to be steaming slightly. I was worried the turtles were going to melt their little mitts right into the tar.

Fortunately, there was a plastic wading pool filled with water and chilling turtles on each side of the track. Kids could choose a favorite filthy turtle from the free-for-all pools or bring their own. It was a zoo, literally and figuratively. Much shrieking and turtle prodding ensued, and twenty minutes later, I was snapping pictures of the winner, Ashley Grosbain, holding her urinating reptile close to her face and grinning. It was sweet, and good birth control.

When I hit Lake Street, hundreds of people were milling around in anticipation of the parade, some carrying treasures from the flea market, others with popcorn from the Big Bopper. The Big Bopper had been driving his popcorn cart into town every July for as long as people could remember. I don't know how he made ends meet. He sold caramel corn, kettle corn, regular popcorn, popcorn balls…if it had popcorn in it, John sold it, but never for more than fifty cents a bag. I didn't need to be a math whiz to figure out he would need to sell a lot of popcorn to even cover his gas money. Not for the first time, I wondered if he was a wealthy eccentric who netted secret joy out of infusing the population with delicious fiber.

The Big Bopper knew me from the previous summers when I had visited Battle Lake to see Sunny, and he never forgot a name. As I walked past his cart, he called out to me, "It's gonna be a busy weekend, Ms. James. Popcorn?"

I declined, but then thought better of it. It's never too early for popcorn. I even bought two sapphire-blue, sugar-soaked popcorn balls to give to the birds back at my place. It might keep them appeased for another day.

I found a good parade-viewing spot directly in front of Ace Hardware and settled myself on the curb between two families just as I heard the cacophonous sound of the high school band break into the opening bars of "Louie, Louie" on the north side of town. The Battle Lake Bulldogs inched their way toward me in hitches and spurts, stopping and starting as directed by their bandleader. By the time they got to me, they had finished "Louie, Louie," segued to "Apache" and then "Wipeout," and were back to "Louie, Louie" again.

Behind the Bulldogs rode the Kiwanis, who hurtled along in their tiny little motorcycles, performing death-defying crazy eights while barely avoiding spectators and each other. They always got my blood racing. A string of convertibles and antique cars followed them, but suddenly, a murmuring passed down the crowd, and I could see people standing up far to the north. This movement passed down the crowd like a wave, until I too was forced to my feet to see what was going on. Bringing up the rear of a 1953 navy blue Chevy were two men, each holding the end of a pole on which hung a "Diversity in Battle Lake" sign. This could only be Kennie's work, a knee-jerk response to Dolly's request for more cultural awareness.

Leading the "diverse" group were three white-skinned men wearing leather Indian outfits straight from a Hollywood wardrobe department, circa 1950. They actually looked like miniature, pale Chief Wenongas without the strength and beauty, and it made me sad. One of them held a sign that said "We Support Native Americans," but they were beating their chests like Tarzan and whooping and hollering. The crowd near me clapped politely. In this area, folks were proud of their hyperliteral rendition of the Chief in the same way they rooted for global warming—quietly, with a good dose of self-flagellation for being so selfish.

Mrs. Berns and her friend Ida followed closely in a golf cart draped with a "Love an Old Lady" banner. Ida looked as crisp as a fall apple, even in this unbearable heat. She wore a white sun visor with a matching tennis dress and shoes, and there was not a curl out of place in her short, white hair. Mrs. Berns was a little less conservative in her Nascar tank top and bike shorts, but the look seemed appropriate, given the speed with which she was driving the golf cart. She apparently was living out her dream of being a Kiwanis.

Holding up the rear were four Klimeks, a family notorious for its farm machinery accidents. All four were dressed in street clothes. One held a sign that said, "Imagine not being able to play video games." The second had a sign that said, "What if you couldn't hitchhike?" The third's sign said, "Envision a life where you can't show approval to someone standing very far away." The fourth, and final, member of this odd troupe had a sign that said, "Support Those Without Thumbs. TWT." The entire group chanted, "Support TWT" as they walked past, and sure enough, all four of them were missing at least one thumb. And that was diversity in Battle Lake.

Before I could get my head around it, the Battle Lake fire truck rolled past, its occupants beaning the crowd with purple taffy and causing children to leave their parents like lemmings toward a cliff, scrambling for pavement-warmed candy. Some more old cars, four really big horses looking lathered in the heat, and what looked like a cheerleading group, followed the fire truck. As they drew closer, I realized it wasn't just any cheerleading group. Kennie Rogers was at the head, and she was wearing her silver can-can dress and stovepipe red, white, and blue hat from yesterday's crime scene. She was accompanied by twelve other women dressed identically, the youngest around fifty, and they were all chanting, "We got spirit, yes we do! We got spirit, how 'bout you? Goooo, Beaver Pelts!"

Between cheers, the baker's dozen of women were handing out business cards. Kennie ran to me and stuffed one in my hand, her cheeks rosy with excitement. "Guess you know what I've been up to, eh Mira? Cheerleading camp! It's called radical cheerleading, and it's the newest way to activate crowds and advertise products in the summer, what with all the parades across the state. You'all could be a Beaver Pelt, too!"

I pulled my hand away as if burned, but I couldn't keep from looking at the card with raised brown letters against a white background.

Radical Cheerleaders for Rent.
Contact Kennie Rogers at beaverpelts@prtel.com
for More Information.

I looked up just in time to see Kennie and her group execute a painfully sexy group hip-grind to Kennie's shouted cheers of "Whoomp, there it is! Whoomp, there it is!"

Kennie was renowned for her odd business endeavors. First she had tried hosting a geriatric party house, then she attempted to push elderly beauty contests with little success, and so she created a gold-panning business on nearby Otter Tail River. I supposed the radical cheerleading shouldn't have been a surprise, but I was having a hard time digesting it.

Before I had a chance to really try, Brando Erikkson's red Humvee roared up on the tails of the Beaver Pelts. The driver pulled the mammoth vehicle to a halt, put it in park, and climbed half-out through the sunroof of the car, megaphone in hand. Kennie rushed from the front of her Pelts so she stood within ten feet of the man. She kept her group dancing what appeared to be a creakily seductive version of Pat Benatar's "Hell Is for Children" music video while they all stared at the Humvee occupant.

In the light of day, he was even more handsome than I had thought from my glimpse of him at Les' Meat and RV and again last night in the dark back streets with Kennie. His black hair, now loose and straight around his shoulders, accented his sharp cheekbones and straight nose, and his smooth smile was dazzlingly white. Apparently, I wasn't the only one who noticed his good looks, as the men around me began grumbling and the women's faces went slack. I wasn't impressed with him, though, if for no other reason than the obnoxious vehicle he drove. Never trust a man who pays for a Hummer.

"Ladies and gentlemen! Hello, and thank you for inviting me to your beautiful town!"

I snapped some shots with the digital, and then angled my head a bit so I could watch him work the crowd. He was good, too. He managed to make visual contact with every woman within distance. His erection eyes slid off one eager face on to the next, and I wondered if he was going to whip out his flute and lead all the women of Battle Lake away like the Pied Piper.

"My name is Brando Erikkson, and my father created the Chief Wenonga statue for your town. Now, it is my understanding that the Chief has gone missing." At his mention of the missing Chief, Brando hung his head, as if saddened. He waited one beat, two beats, three, then lifted his head and blinded the crowd with his grin. "But I have good news! Fibertastic Enterprises is going to donate a slightly irregular woodchuck to grace your beautiful town until the Chief is returned!"

Kennie squealed and applauded, and soon, the whole crowd was cheering good-naturedly. Brando threw his hands in the air as if signaling a victory.

A woodchuck? That was slightly irregular?

I was distracted from the rest of Brando's speech as the golf cart that had carried Ida and Mrs. Berns came roaring back against the grain of the parade. Mrs. Berns was no longer in the cart, and an addled-looking Ida was yelling, "Someone stole the Indian! The Indian is gone!"

She was largely ignored as everyone stared, rapt, at Brando in his Humvee. The woman next to me muttered, "The old coot just figured out someone stole Chief Wenonga?"

I glared at the woman and rushed out to Ida, worried she was suffering from heat stroke. When I reached the cart, I placed my hand over hers and pulled her foot off the pedal. "Are you OK, Ida? Is it the temperature?"

She looked at me, her eyes blazing. "Someone stole the Indian!"

"Shh, shh, Ida. It's OK. The police are looking for Chief Wenonga. It'll be OK." I could hear Brando mesmerizing the crowd through his megaphone but couldn't pay attention to the words. I turned my head to holler for an ambulance, but not before the panic in Ida's voice cut through the thick summer air and forced me to look back at her.

"It's not the Wenonga statue. It was Bill Myers, one of the Indian impersonators from the parade. He's been kidnapped!"

ELEVEN

MY KNEES WENT WEAK, and I dropped myself into the shaded seat next to Ida. "What do you mean, kidnapped?"

"I mean, he was there, talking to me and Mrs. Berns, and then he was gone. The other two Indians don't know where he went. He's been taken by ghosts!"

"I'm sure there is a rational explanation. He probably just went into the Rusty Nail for a beer." I felt my heartbeat slow down.

She set her shoulders stubbornly. "He was supposed to go with the other two Indians to the head of the parade and walk back down again. Kennie wanted the parade to end with Indians. He's disappeared."

Sure enough, as Brando pulled himself back into his Humvee, his speech apparently over, and the Beaver Pelts faced front again, I noticed two confused-looking guys in Indian costumes straggling behind the mammoth red vehicle. They were scanning the crowd and shrugging.

"I'm sure it's fine, Ida. Why don't you go tell Gary Wohnt what's going on? I bet they'll find Mr. Myers real soon."

She looked doubtful, but after I slipped out of the cart, she drove off toward the police station. For my part, I jogged down the street the half mile or so to the Meat and RV shop, stopping at the end of the parade route to buy a bottle of icy water from a kid with a cooler. I didn't know if Les was capable of kidnapping a statue *and* a man, but if he had taken Bill Myers, he wouldn't have gotten far.

I cruised to the back of the shop, out of breath and sweaty. Before I checked for Les, I chugged some cold water, pressing the chilled bottle against my face after I capped it. I knew the Meat and RV store was closed for the holiday, but when I yanked on the back door, it opened smoothly. Surprised, I walked in without pausing, washed in the smell of smoked meat and car oil. The back room looked exactly like I expected—open pizza boxes falling over piles of newspaper, dingy gray file cabinets half open, overflowing ashtrays heaped in corners. This place was a fire hazard and far too messy to snoop in. A computer printout on the top of a mound of newspapers caught my eye because of its whiteness. I glanced quickly at it, noting "University of Wisconsin" printed across the top. It appeared to be a hard copy of Dr. Dolly Castle's web page. It featured a photo of her smiling sedately, a list of the Native American Indian classes she would be teaching in the fall and their syllabi, and contact information.

Underneath it was a printout from another website with a laminated card paperclipped to it. The website was called "The Man's Militia," and the front page listed a statement of grievances against the United States federal government. The next page listed adversaries of the militia, but it was all general references to corrupt bureaucrats, law enforcement agencies, judges, and prosecutors. The laminated card attached to it had a grainy photo of Les Pastner, sans hat, his full name—Lester Luther Pastner—his vital statistics, and a picture of a red flag featuring a blue "x" dotted with eleven white stars over the words "The Independent States of America." I glanced around for a computer but didn't see one.

I strode purposefully to the front before I lost my adrenaline boner. This was the part of the store the customers saw, and it smelled cool and peppery. There was one refrigerated display case about the size of a couch next to the cash register, and it was packed with shrink-wrapped beef, sausages, and jerky. In the far corner, an old-fashioned metal desk was stacked neatly with Winnebago brochures. The corkboard to the left of the front door was covered in notices for auctions, garage sales, and free kittens.

Other than the furniture, the room was empty, which left only one place to explore. Behind the till, directly next to the doorway leading to the back room I had just come out of, was a closed door made of the cheap wood found in prefabricated homes. I turned around and walked to this door, the cockiness melting out of my step. It occurred to me that I was trespassing in the workspace of a questionably unstable militia man who had begun to wear a hat about the same time a piece of scalp had shown up at the base of the stolen Chief Wenonga.

I forced myself forward, leaving a trail of cooling nerve behind me. One step, two steps, three steps, and the cool metal of the doorknob was in my hand. One turn, push, and I was in the windowless room. My eyes adjusted in seconds, and I moved forward into what could be generously described as a living space. There was an aging TV against one wall, its antennae covered in twisted tin foil. Next to the television was an open door that looked in on a toilet and sink. On the far wall of the room stood a card table with a gimpy leg and two folding chairs. The next wall over was consumed by a couch, and someone was sprawled on it. I stepped back involuntarily, an image of finding Jeff's body in the library slapping me across both cheeks.

In fact, this body was laid out just like Jeff's, with the arms crossed and a hat instead of a book covering the face. I forced myself forward, my legs creaking stiffly. I reached down and toward the hat, the smell of smoked meat overwhelming all my senses. I noticed distantly that it was the Cenex cap I had seen Les wearing last night. I felt as if I was swimming through Vaseline, pushing toward the green bill of the cap. My fingers grasped the smooth cloth, and I pulled the hat gently away and screamed.

TWELVE

LES PASTNER WAS UNDER the hat, and he slept with his eyes open. He looked like a lizard-man. How did his peepers not dry out? My scream startled him awake, and he jumped off the couch, pulling a shotgun from the crease between the back and seat cushions.

"I am ready. What in the hell, I am ready!"

I jumped back and threw my hands over my head. "It's me, Les! Mira! From the library. You can put the gun down."

Les kept his head moving, searching for enemies in the corners. When he found only me, he lowered the gun and scratched his head. It was then I noticed he'd been the recipient of a really bad haircut that left him bald in spots but otherwise completely intact.

"Whaddya want, Mira?"

I lowered my hands. "I just have a couple questions, Mr. Pastner. For the paper. Do you have a minute?" Having a gun pointed at me made me feel like throwing up, but I needed to take advantage of the situation. I lowered my shaking body into a chair and realized I had no idea what to ask him.

"Jeezus. You scared me near half to death." He scratched at his head, his close-set eyes still looking erratically around the room. Up close, he reminded me a little of Mickey Rooney.

"Yeah, likewise."

"You should know better than to sneak up on a man like that. It's probably best you go."

"Just a couple questions, Mr. Pastner. What was Brando Erikkson doing here last night?"

Les ran his fingers over the bristly peaks and valleys of his haircut and reached down for his hat. "We was working out a business deal."

"About what?"

"About none of your business."

"Are you bothered that Chief Wenonga is gone?"

Les walked over to me and made a shooing motion. "I already talked to the police about Chief Wenonga. I sell Meat and RVs, not statues. Got no use for 'em."

I had no choice but to stand, but I took my own sweet time moving toward the door. "Did you know that another Indian disappeared today, this one a real human from the parade?"

That gave Les pause. "When was that?"

"Not fifteen minutes ago."

"Well, you saw me, here, asleep. Right?"

"Just now, yeah, but I don't know what you were doing fifteen minutes ago."

Les stopped herding me out and reappraised me. "Well, maybe we can make a deal. Maybe I can tell you something about Chief Wenonga gone missing, and you can remember you've been here for fifteen minutes."

I crossed my fingers behind my back. "Sure. What do you know about Chief Wenonga?"

"I know Dr. Dolly Castle been in town for two days, and if what you say about the parade today is true, two Indians have gone missing in as many days. That's the tree you should be barking up."

"Are you saying Dolly knows where Chief Wenonga is?"

"I'm saying you should keep your eye on her."

That was a pretty lame quid pro quo, but since I had no intention of lying for Les, I suppose it was a fair exchange. He apparently thought we were done because he was shooing me out again.

"You know where Brando is staying?"

"A cabin right north of town." Up this close, Les smelled lonely, like the inside of a pumpkin.

"What about Dr. Dolly Castle? Where's she staying?"

"She's out at the motel."

Now I was completely outside, the bright sunlight all but melting my skin. "So you didn't take the Chief."

Les Pastner looked me squarely in the eye. "I have no idea where Chief Wenonga is."

I had enough experience with the gray side of the truth to know I had just been blown off with a non-lie, but before I could follow up, Les had slammed the door in my face and slid the lock loudly into place. It was then that I heard the sirens coming toward me. I was exposed, with a closed metal door in front of me and the nearest cover a fleet of rusty Winnebagoes forty feet away. I opted for false bravado and strolled toward town, the bill of my borrowed Twins hat tugged low. As the sirens approached, my strides grew longer. I could almost see the navy blue of the squad cars by the time the RVs were ten feet away, and I couldn't keep my cool any longer. I squealed like a boy and dove under an ancient GMC Mini Jimmy Motorhome, scraping both knees, just as a police car tore out of town on 78 and ripped up 210 toward Fergus Falls. Something big had just happened in Battle Lake.

THIRTEEN

I DUSTED MYSELF OFF and made my way back toward town, the gravel-studded skin over my knees pulling painfully with every step. The initial people I encountered were throngs of happy tourists carrying Larry's Grocery bags weighted down with cheap parade candy. Gina was the first person I recognized, her familiar white-blonde hair shining in the sun, as she huffed her short, round body to Granny's Pantry.

Gina and Sunny had been good friends before Sunny split for Alaska, and I had picked up where Sunny had left off. Gina was an enormous blonde nurse with the heart of a randy saint. Her husband, Leif, was a philanderer, but he had stayed true ever since I had innocently happened upon some damning photos snapped of him and Kennie one night when he'd had one too many.

"Mira? Is that you under there?" Gina tapped at the Twins hat and grinned at me, her smile brightening her fleshy face. "You look like a dork. What in the hell are you doing in that cap?"

"It's yours, dork. No time to talk. Do you know why the police just zipped out of town?"

"You haven't heard? There's been a kidnapping. Someone grabbed Billy Myers from the parade. He was one of the guys dressed like an Indian. I tell you, it doesn't pay to be an Indian in Battle Lake right about now."

"At least not a fake one. They're sure he isn't just out tying one on somewhere?"

Gina dug her hand into her purse and came out with a packet of Laffy Taffy. She wasn't afraid to talk with her mouth full. "Pretty sure. He's a reliable guy, and he's disappeared. The cops are a little jumpy, anyhow, but two missing Indians in two days isn't good."

I shook my head in agreement. "You got any other dirt?"

Gina raised her eyebrows suggestively at me. "You mean dirt, like the kind Johnny Leeson was throwing around at his Community Ed class today?"

For a second, I let myself go there, to a world where Johnny and I gardened together. A picture of his lean upper body bending over a hotbed of sprouts blissfully decorated the corners of my mind. His hair would fall into his eyes, and I'd rush to his side to push it away. He'd smile at me, stop my hand halfway to his face, and tell me that he could no longer bear his life without spending some quality time in my loins. I'd demur, for a second, and then he'd throw me over his shoulder and carry me out to the garden patch for a little irrigating.

"Mira? I was kidding about Johnny. Mira?"

I focused guiltily back on Gina, who had moved on to Tootsie Rolls. Had I been drooling? I decided not to tell her about my pending date tonight. I didn't want to jinx it. "Of course you were, Gina. I was just thinking about how weird this town's been."

"You mean lately? Or since the 1800s?"

"Ha ha."

"You want to go to the fireworks with Leif and me tonight?" I had forgotten about the fireworks. They might be a good opportunity to dig up more information, as long as it didn't interfere with my Johnny time. "Maybe. What time you going?"

"We're meeting some people for drinks at Stub's at 8:00 and heading to Glendalough at 9:30 or so. The fireworks are supposed to start at 10:00."

"I don't feel like Stub's. How 'bout I just look for you at Glendalough, by the pay stand, around 9:45?" Glendalough was a gorgeous state park north of town. It consisted of nearly two thousand acres of pristine prairie lands and six lakes within its borders, donated to the Nature Conservancy by the Cowles Family on Earth Day, 1990, and then passed over to the Minnesota Department of Natural Resources two years later. It was a favorite location for Fourth of July fireworks viewing, which were traditionally launched from the shores of Molly Stark Lake within its borders.

"Deal. Bring a blanket and mosquito repellent. And I've got some big news."

Probably she was getting her ears pierced for a sixth time. She gave me a quick hug and headed in the direction of home, and I took off for the library. I moaned when I stepped inside, the air conditioning feeling like a massage on my hot skin. Some hair had escaped from my bun and lay like hot snakes against my neck, and I tied this back up before heading to the bathroom to wash up my raw palms and knees.

Once I was clean and cool, I typed up my article, which was already over an hour past deadline. I didn't have much to add to the original, except a new closing paragraph:

In a surprising turn of events, Bill Myers has disappeared from the Fourth of July parade. At the time of his capture, Mr. Myers was dressed as a Native American, similar in garb to the Chief Wenonga statue. The similarities between the cases have police baffled. Maybe these males are asking for it by the way they dress? Regardless, the police are currently investigating the missing statue and Myers and hope to have both returned safely.

While I was online, I searched for information on Fibertastic Enterprises. The first hit showed a one-page website featuring various fiberglass statues, chief among them my Wenonga. That was all there was, besides contact information. According to the site, Fibertastic Enterprises was located in Stevens Point, Wisconsin, a town about three hours southeast of St. Paul. There was a phone number and email address, both of which I jotted down.

I shut off the computer, locked up the library, and headed upstream against the parade lingerers, intent on finding out more about Dolly. When I reached the twelve-room, log-sided Battle Lake Motel, it was readily apparent that there was no red Humvee around, though there was no reason there should have been other than a nagging hunch I had that Dolly and Brando knew each other. I wasn't sure what kind of car Dolly drove, but the only vehicle in the entire lot with Wisconsin license plates was a black Honda Civic plastered in bumper stickers like, "Keep your laws off my body," "Virginia is for lovers," "Indians discovered America," and "The first boat people were white." I peeked in the car windows and saw some littered Coca Cola cans and a stack of CDs. Must be Dolly's.

I entered the front office of the motel and pretended to admire the prints of ducks and dogs in the waiting space while the young woman working the front desk spoke on the phone. When she was free, I asked her if she knew what room Dolores Castle was staying in.

She smiled kindly at me. "I'm afraid I can't give out personal information about our guests, but I'd happy to give Miss Castle a message for you."

"Can you tell me if that's her Honda Civic out front?"

The young woman's smile faltered. "I'm afraid that's against motel policy. Sorry."

I scanned my brain for ways to trick her out of the information but came up with nothing. I figured my best bet was to wait on the fringes of the Halvorson flea market adjacent to the hotel until either Brando Erikkson or Dolly came by, or it was time to get ready for my Johnny time, so I thanked her and headed back into the early afternoon heat.

I sidled up to the nearest flea market table which, near as I could tell, sold the contents of various junk drawers from over the ages—rusty doorknobs, cheap Marlboro lighters, assorted tintype photos, pocket knives. All the stuff that you don't want even when you own it. I pretended to dig through the crusty treasure as I counted the minutes, and then the hours. The white-haired man running the booth gave up trying to sell me something about 3:00 PM. At 3:30, I'd had enough and was turning to go home when I caught a glimpse of a strawberry blonde walking down the motel walkway toward a room.

I tried to stroll away unobtrusively, furtively sniffing at the metallic smell of my fingers, stained orange from digging in junk. I would need to wash these puppies. I ducked down as the reddish-blonde head turned toward me, and through the windows of the car I was hiding behind, I affirmed it was Dolly. She looked flushed and happy. She was in and out of her room, a golden "7" on its door, in under three minutes. She hurried to the black Civic and peeled out of the parking lot before I could say "hi."

I walked casually to her door. A quick twist of the knob told me it had locked automatically behind her, and the shades were closed tightly on her windows. Where had she been off to in such a hurry, and what had made her so happy?

I started back toward my car, still parked at Gina's, and then had a flash. Should I stop by the drugstore to prepare myself for my meeting with Johnny? It probably wasn't an official date, and even if it was, I technically didn't want to date right now, and even if I did, we probably weren't going to fool around. But it sure would suck to be pregnant by accident. I decided I had nothing to lose from a quick trip to the Apothecary. If nothing else, it wouldn't be the first pack of condoms to expire, lonely and unused, in my bedside stand.

There was only one problem with this plan. Buying condoms is never fun, but in a small town where everyone knows your business, it can be horrifying. For an example of the small town gossip train, last month, I ordered a caffeine-free Coke instead of my usual Classic Coke with my lunch at the Turtle Stew. Three hours later, Gina phoned me at the library to ask if I was pregnant. Because of this wicked closeness in Battle Lake, I was always careful to keep my business private as much as possible. There was no way around the condom issue, though, so I walked purposefully into the Apothecary and straight to the condom aisle.

There was a huge variety, but I had long ago decided choosing which condom to buy was like picking which dish to order at a Mexican restaurant—they might have different names, but they're all the same. I grabbed the pack nearest me and headed toward the counter, where Johnny Leeson was buying some sort of medicine and a bag of balloons, his back to me. My cheeks burned with imminent shame.

I concealed the condoms behind my back, not sure if Johnny would think I was presumptuous, slutty, or well-prepared if he noticed them. I carefully backed away until I was behind the end cap suntan lotion display, where I dropped the condoms like a bundle of itchweed. I grabbed the nearest magazine off the rack and walked back around.

"Hi, Johnny," I said, feigning casual.

He turned quickly, and then moved to shield his purchases while the cashier bagged them. "Hey, Mira." He looked embarrassed, and as soon as the cashier handed him his bag, he hurried toward the door. "See you tonight!"

I shook my head. Was even Johnny going weird on me? I glanced absently at the magazine I had grabbed, noting it was *Cosmo*, the intelligent woman's kryptonite. I had long ago decided I would rather be strong than skinny, and to that end, I avoided glossy mags. I was about to return it when the splashy line on the cover caught my eye: "First Date Fears? Make Yourself Sweet and Sassy so He'll Love You Forever." Was it a sign, an arrow piercing a red heart, pointing from Johnny to me? I paid for the magazine, stashing it under my arm so no one would see me with it.

Once home, some quality pet time was my first order of business. I walked Luna the half mile to the mailbox and back, reminding her every few feet that she was a good dog. She needed that constant reinforcement. Tiger Pop, on the other hand, followed discreetly behind us, sticking to the shade and just coincidentally going the same direction. Back at the double-wide, I scratched them both behind their ears and refilled their water bowls, again adding ice. I hopped into the shower to cool off. The clear and cool water felt great cutting through the dirt and sweat coating me from the day's exertions.

I stepped out and bandaged my knees, clean but sore from the RV dive, and made myself a light snack of sliced gouda cheese and apples. I pulled out the *Cosmo* to read while my hair dried. The "First Date Fears?" article was on page 217, sandwiched between an ad for perfume and an ad for diamonds. I clearly was not their target audience.

OK, you've been chasing Mr. Dreamboat for weeks, and you've finally caught him! Now what do you do? Make yourself sweet and sassy of course! Don't waste your time or his by showing up to this date less than fantabulous. Follow these five easy steps to make the night magically memorable. And who knows? It just might lead to marriage:

1. Rinse your hair with egg and beer. It'll make it shiny, shimmery, and irresistible! Trust us when we tell you he won't be able to keep his hands off of it.

2. Paint your lips red. This will incite his animal instincts and draw attention to what you are saying. Make sure you ask him lots of questions about himself!

3 . Dab a little vanilla oil behind each ear. A way to a man's heart is through his stomach, and you just might be the tastiest treat he'll eat!

4. Actually, most women aren't as tasty and fresh as they'd like to be. To "sweeten the pot" once you've drawn him in, drink at least four cups of pineapple juice before you two decide to get jiggy. It'll keep him coming back for more!

5. And finally, don't eat anything that can get stuck in your teeth. Stick to low-fat, low-carb, leaf-free dishes like carrots, boiled chicken, and lean steak. When he smiles at you, he doesn't want to see the broccoli smiling back!

I threw the magazine down, disgusted. Women had earned the right to vote in 1920 and eighty years later had apparently traded it in for the freedom to be cute. I walked over to the fridge for some cold water and saw the can of Miller Lite in the back, a leftover from Sunny's tenure. Next to that was a carton with a half dozen brown eggs. I looked from *Cosmo* back to the inside of my fridge. Well, there was nothing wrong with having shiny hair, I told myself. And I wouldn't be doing it for Johnny, I'd be doing it for me.

I grabbed an egg and the beer, cracked both, and whipped them together in a bowl. I leaned my head over the kitchen sink and poured the slimy, fizzy mess onto my nearly dry hair. The article hadn't mentioned how long to leave it in, so I stayed put for eleven—my lucky number—minutes. When I couldn't stand it any longer, I turned on the tap and rinsed out the glop until the water ran clear, and then bundled it up in a towel turban on my head.

In for a penny, in for a pound. I rummaged through my make-up drawer and finally came up with some crusty old rouge that I dabbed on my lips. It was more liver pink than lover red, but hopefully wherever we were eating would be poorly lit. I had less luck finding vanilla oil. As a compromise, I grabbed the bottle of 100% vanilla extract from my spice rack and dabbed a little on each wrist and behind each ear. It was sticky, but I smelled like cookies. I knew I didn't have pineapple juice and wasn't going to order boiled chicken tonight, so I'd just have to stop at half crazy.

I was trying to regain some self-respect by reminding myself how I didn't want to date because all men went bad or dead on me when Johnny pulled up. He had been to my house once before, in June, to help me do some landscaping. I thought we had made a connection that night, but I was either too afraid or too smart to pursue it. I was wondering if tonight would tip that balance.

I let my hair out of the towel and quickly brushed it. It was damp but would dry quickly in the heat. I had visions of it drying and plumping into a perfect, sassy and sexy Barbarella-do. I patted Tiger Pop and Luna goodbye and loped out to meet Johnny. He smiled when he saw me, the sun making a halo of gold around his sun-browned face. He opened the door for me and I glided in. When he slid in his side, I could see his dimples carving out a little space on each cheek.

"What?"

"Nothing."

"What?"

Johnny put the car into first and took off down the driveway. "You smell like a beer hall and have something yellow on your shoulder."

I looked down, mortified. "Oh, um, it's a new shampoo. Beer shampoo. Beer and egg. Yolk."

"Really?"

"I got it at the store." I swatted at a fly buzzing around my head, but the movement of my wrist just attracted another.

"Are you OK if we eat at Stub's?"

"That'd be great." Suddenly, there was a swarm of heat-drunk flies around me. Were they after the beer and egg in my hair? I swung again and caught a whiff of vanilla. Christ. I had turned myself into fly bait. I should have just rubbed some raw hamburger under each armpit and called it a night. I shoved my vanilla-dabbed hands under my legs and tried to wipe at the sweetness under each ear with my shoulder. Johnny watched out of the corner of his eye, a smile tugging at his lip. When flies buzzed close, I blew at them out of the side of my mouth, hoping the radio covered up the sound. *Cosmo* sure was right: I was making a memorable impression on this first date.

As soon as we got into Stub's Dining Hall, I excused myself and went to the bathroom. I was able to scour the vanilla and scrape most of the egg drippings off my shoulders. My hair, however, had dried and was now irreparably crusty and not reflecting any light. Fortunately, I always carried a hair band with me. Once I pulled it up and back and scrubbed the uneven, ailing pink off my lips, I felt slightly better. I still smelled like a beer hall, but at least I was *in* a beer hall.

Johnny was waiting for me at the bar, a teasing smile still playing across his lips. He didn't comment on my changed appearance. "I got us the last table, Mira, but they need to clear it off first. Can I get you a drink?"

I had decided in the bathroom that this wasn't a date, if for no other reason than to save my sanity, and so was sticking with my plan of crossing number four off the *Cosmo* list. "A Coke would be nice."

The bartender nodded, and Johnny reached for his wallet. Out of the blue, Heaven, in all her clean-haired, immaculately made-up, youthful glory, popped up next to him. "Johnny! I'm here with some friends of my brother's from college. They say they know you. You should come sit with us!"

Johnny put his hand firmly on my waist, and my side tingled where he touched it. "I'm with Mira."

I quickly leaned over to the bartender. "Can you make that a pineapple juice?"

Heaven pouted. "Whatever. Maybe we can all hook up at the fireworks later."

"Maybe." Johnny smiled agreeably, grabbed our drinks, and let me lead the way into the dining room. Our table was relatively private in the crowded room, set back in a space like a closet with hanging curtains instead of a door on the front. We studied our menus inside the curtained alcove. We both ordered—steak for Johnny and chicken for me—before he told me the real reason he had asked me out.

"I have a favor to ask of you."

That didn't sound like one potential lover to another. I stared miserably at my salad, wondering if I had indeed turned him off by ordering something leafy.

"I'm going out of town for a few days, and I need someone to watch my place."

I hoped I hid the disappointment on my face with a good cover of confusion. "House sit? But aren't you still at your mom's place?" When Johnny came over to help me in June, I had learned that he had been starting grad school in Wisconsin when he got word his dad was diagnosed with terminal stomach cancer. He returned to Battle Lake to help his mom take care of his dad and was making the best of his current life working at the nursery, giving piano lessons, teaching community ed classes, and being the town handyman. His dad had died around the same time I arrived in Battle Lake, and Johnny was staying on another year to make sure his mom was situated. He was an only child, like me.

"Yeah, but I'm working on my cabin out on the west side of Silver Lake. I think some kids were partying out there last night, spinning ueys in the driveway. The locks are still on the door, but I don't know for how long, especially if they get wind that I'm out of town."

"Couldn't Jed watch it?"

"Jed's a great guy, but not what you'd call reliable."

"Sure, I suppose." I frowned. "You just want me to drive out there every day?"

"Easier than that. All you need to do is keep your eyes peeled for a car with red paint on it."

"Huh? A red car?"

"No, a car with red paint on it. I filled some balloons with paint and put them in the dried-up mud puddles in my driveway. They're covered with leaves, and anyone driving at night won't be able to see them. Whoever is tearing up the driveway is going to have a car full of red paint splatters."

"Isn't that a little vengeful for you?"

Johnny ducked his eyes. "My dad and I built that cabin. It's fallen apart since I've been to college and he was sick, and I'm just getting it back together. I don't want it trashed."

"I'm sorry. Of course I'll watch for the red paint. You just want me to call the police if I see something?"

"I want you to call me. I can be back within a few hours."

"Where are you going?"

The waitress took our salad plates away, distracting Johnny's gaze. "Wisconsin. Stevens Point, actually. To visit my grandma."

"Hunh." I watched Johnny watching the waitress and wondered why he was suddenly unable to make eye contact with me. If I didn't know him better, I'd say he was telling me a big fat fib. I tried remembering where he had told Dolly and me his grandparents lived when he had run into us at the Fortune Café, but the beer fumes cloaking my head discouraged clear thinking.

Johnny nodded. "Yup."

"When are you leaving?"

"Tonight. When we're done with supper."

For sure no lovin' for me tonight. "On the Fourth of July? What's the rush?"

Johnny rubbed his palms on his pants. "Sure is taking our food a long time."

"Sure is."

"Yup."

"Yup."

"Yeah, no rush, really. I just thought I'd go see my grandma tonight, beat the weekend traffic. Can we talk about something else?"

What I wanted to talk about was how Johnny was turning into a great big liar, just like the rest of them. Instead, I sipped at my saccharine-sweet pineapple juice and wondered if Johnny's uneasiness had anything to do with the missing Chief Wenonga, the bloody scalp, or the missing parade Indian. I made myself a promise to check out his cabin and see what this booby-trapping paint balloon dealio was really about in the very near future.

FOURTEEN

My non-date supper finished uneventfully. Johnny drove me home so I could grab my own wheels to have at the fireworks. He flashed me an unusually shy smile when he opened the car door for me. Of course, it could have just been the beer fumes still wafting from my tapped keg of hair that made him look uncomfortable. As we said our goodbyes, he told me he would call me when he returned if I didn't call him on his cell first.

I considered biking to the fireworks at Glendalough Park to keep a low profile. However, Fourth of July traffic is notoriously dangerous since people are excited, drunk, and looking at the sky. It's a bad time to be on a bike, so I reluctantly drove my Toyota to the park on the north side of town, hoping the gravel dust blanketing it would make it indistinguishable from other cars in the deepening dusk. With my windows down, I could hear the frogs sighing and the crickets singing in the fragrant sloughs hugging the road. The cooling evening breeze felt like a soft kiss on the baby hairs of my neck, and I began to get excited at the thought of fireworks.

My family rarely made it to the Fourth of July festivities when I was younger. My dad was usually drunk by dark, and before I hit the age of ten, my mom had started going to bed early to avoid him. I had spent every Fourth of July that I could remember perched on the slouched metal roof of the storage shed on our tiny hobby farm in the middle of the flat, west-central Minnesota prairie. I couldn't see the real fireworks streaking through the sky above Lake Koronis, six miles away, but I could hear them, and I could see our neighbors shoot off Roman candles smuggled in from North Dakota. Every time I heard a pop, I'd throw handfuls of tree helicopters into the air, or grass clippings.

I soon outgrew the Fourth of July on the roof and was left to watch fireworks on the little black and white TV in our living room, for as long as I could put up with my dad's drunken commentary on everything from the problems with me to the woman he should have married. Now, as a grown-up, watching real fireworks was like reclaiming the childhood I never had. This would be the fifth summer I had seen the fireworks in Battle Lake, thanks to Sunny.

I knew the parking would be impossible in Glendalough, and even worse trying to leave after the fireworks, so I joined a sprinkling of parked cars at the mouth of the park. I fell in line with the crowds all the way to the pay booth where park guests were asked to donate if they didn't already own a Minnesota State Park sticker.

On the far side of the large map and interpretive sign, I almost missed Dolly walking in. She still had the lighthearted step and distant smile of a happy woman, and I was about to holler at her when I noticed Les hot on her heels. I think he thought he was blending in with the crowd, but with the angry set of his shoulders and the grimace on his face, he stood out like a snake in a baby crib. When Dolly stopped quickly to smell a tiger lily sprouting up amid the prairie grass, Les stopped also and dropped down, pretending to tie his shoe. Did Dolly know she was being followed, and why was Les following her?

I was about to become the third car on that train when Gina popped up alongside me.

"There you are! How long have you been here?"

Gina wore a shapeless, patriotic T-shirt, blue-jeans, and flip-flops. Her thin blonde hair was pulled back in a pony tail, and her bright green eyes smiled at me.

"Just got here. So, what's your big news?"

"Let's walk and talk." Gina hooked her arm through mine and navigated me around the jostling crowds over to a choice spot on the banks of Molly Stark Lake.

"We're walking, but we're not talking." I was studying the crowds, trying to catch a glimpse of Dolly, but I wasn't oblivious to the fact that Gina was unusually quiet.

She stopped dead in her tracks and faced me. "OK, Mira, don't be mad at me, but I'm pregnant."

My initial thought was *ohmygod, better her than me*, but my sporadically effective social filter managed to click down in the nick of time. I grabbed her up in a big hug. "Mad? Why would I be mad? You're going to be a fantastic mom!"

Gina laughed and pushed me off. "I know how you feel about Leif, but he's changed. He swore he'll never cheat again, and he's changed. He's excited for the baby."

My eyes misted over. I didn't know whether or not Leif had or would change, but I knew that Gina was a whole lot braver than I would ever be. I had decided that being single was like being fat; if society let me get away with it, it'd be my preferred method of existence. I'm not talking "need to remove a wall from your house to heave you out when you die" fat. I'm talking "eat until you're full and then have a piece of cake with ice cream" fat. A girl could dream.

"I'm sure he is excited. I hope this is everything you want it to be."

Gina squeezed my hand, sniffing at the air. "Did someone spill a beer on you? You reek."

"New shampoo."

"You know, Mir, they say pregnancy is contagious. Once one friend gets it, they all do." I could hear the teasing in her voice. "You're on birth control, right?"

"Ha! That'd be like wearing a parachute while you're driving. Is that Leif over there?"

We wove through the crowd to the blanket Leif had set out for the three of us. I said my greetings and allowed myself to be introduced to the two couples Gina and Leif came with. From what I could tell from an initial glance, both were from the heavy-drinking and TV-watching stock, the women sporting 80s claw hair and the men condescending and dumb. It was only an odd combination if you'd never been west of the Twin Cities. I'd tolerated this type of people when I had to, but when one of the guys, who was coincidentally sporting a Long Hard Johnson Fishing Poles T-shirt, asked Leif if he'd ever heard the joke about how you can't rely on a woman because you should never trust anything that bleeds for seven days and doesn't die, I decided it was time to look for greener pastures.

I stood, brushed myself off, and said goodbye to Gina. It was going to be hard to find Dolly among the crowd since it had grown dark. There were hundreds of blankets covered with couples and families dotting the shoreline. No alcohol was allowed within the park limits, but people were openly swigging beer. I decided it would be the best use of my time to hit the far end of the lakeshore and work my way back in an inward pattern, walking along the beach and then backtracking one layer in, until I had worked myself between every group of people. Of course I'd only find Dolly if she had situated herself in this prime firework-viewing location. If she wasn't on Molly Stark, or if Les had knocked her over the head and dragged her into the woods, I was SOL.

I caught snatches of conversation as I walked through the crowds, punctuated by the first, sparkling fireworks lighting up the sky.

"Oooh! That looked like a purple mushroom!"

"When I was a kid, the fireworks blew up in shapes, like flags or George Washington's profile."

"Did you bring the Boone's Farm?"

"You gotta emphasize the *Boone's*, not the *Farm*, man, or it just sounds gross."

"Wow! That lit up the whole night!"

"Think they'll have one shaped like Chief Wenonga?"

I was at the far end of the crowd, trying not to get distracted by the beautiful rainbow reflections of the fireworks shimmering on the lake. It was when I was pulling my gaze away from the water that I caught sight of a couple, thirty feet up the shore on a little stretch of beach almost too narrow to stand on, the water on one side and marshy reeds on the other. I waited for the next explosion to light up the sky before I could see who it was. In a flash of brilliant red, white, and blue, I clearly made out Dolly's signature reddish-blonde hair and the dark silhouette of a tattoo on her right wrist, but the person standing next to her was obscured in shadows.

It was a masculine figure, taller than Dolly, leaning down to talk to her. Whether his hair was light or dark, I couldn't tell. Either way, Dolly was happy to have him close, so I was pretty sure it wasn't Les, who was shorter than Dolly anyway. I casually strolled closer, dropping down on my haunches when Dolly looked my way. When I reached the edge of the reeds, about twenty feet from where the couple was standing and away from the bulk of the fireworks crowd, I could make out bits of conversation floating over the water.

"…for another week or so."

"You sure that's right?"

"I'm positive." Dolly's deep chuckle. "You think I have what it takes?"

"…up to you…"

I risked a peek around the reeds. Dolly's back was to me, but her companion was looking in my direction. I quickly darted back behind the reeds, but not before Johnny Leeson's eyes locked on mine. He was out with Dolly, and he had seen me spying on them.

"Mira?" he called out, but I was already jogging toward my car.

FIFTEEN

I WAS PISSED. OFF. I was mad at Johnny for not being in love with me, even though he was turning out to be a sneak, and I was furious at Dolly for horning in on my territory. The argument could be made that she didn't know I was interested in Johnny, but I wasn't in the mood for generosity. Mostly, though, I was mad at myself for falling for another guy. Love always ended badly for me. I couldn't even fall for a fiberglass statue without it ending poorly, for the love of Betsy.

I was so caught up in my dark mood that I didn't notice Brando stroll out of the woods, and I walked smack into him.

"Oh! Sorry." This was my first face-to-face encounter with him, and based on the carnivorous once-over he gave me, he seemed to be enjoying it a great deal more than I was.

"Not a problem. Where are you going in such a hurry?" He grinned and winked.

"I'm not a big fan of fireworks."

"Mmm." He beckoned over my shoulder. "See anything interesting back there?"

From where we stood, I could see the outlines of hundreds of people staring up at the sky over by the beach, but there was no foot traffic near us, and the closest blanket of people was a few hundred yards away. Feeling slightly uneasy, I swatted at a mosquito and went from defense to offense.

"Just bright lights in the sky. What about you? What are you doing back here?"

He laughed and held out his hand. "I don't think we've met. I'm Brando Erikkson. I'm in town for the festivities."

I shook his hand reluctantly, noting his smoothly manicured nails and strong fingers. "Mira James."

A light of recognition flared in his eyes. "Sure. You've got that column. Kennie mentioned you."

I'll bet. "So, *you* see anything interesting back there?"

"Not much. There's a path down to the lake, but some young lovers were making the most of the night, so I turned back."

Ouch. "Well, it was nice meeting you."

"Some of us are having a party after the show. You should join us." He laid a light hand on my shoulder. "Maybe you could do an article on me."

"Yeah, maybe." I pushed his hand off my shoulder and stomped off. The party would probably be a good place to gather more information on the missing Chief, but I was in no mood. I located my car without spotting any law enforcement and rolled home.

I fell into a funky sleep right away and awoke to a bright ,shining fifth of July, my head pounding from a broken-heart hangover. I didn't feel like eating breakfast, or cleaning, or watching TV, or

111

gardening, or doing anything else I normally do to pull myself out of a dark mood. That left only mowing the lawn, all one and a half acres.

I don't enjoy the actual act of mowing the lawn, but I love the clean smell of fresh-cut grass and the soft, trimmed carpet of green afterward. I strolled down to the outbuilding where I stored the mower, listening to fuzzy bumblebees the size of peanut M & Ms buzzing against the petals of my summer flowers. I gassed up the old Snapper rider, checked the oil, and yanked the whipcord. The engine fired immediately, and I began the bumpy job of trimming the grass. I divided the lawn into segments. First, I mowed the area between the silo, barn, and two sheds. Then, I trimmed the strip running parallel to the mile-long driveway and the tiny beach area down by the lake, and I finally cleared off the wide section circumscribing the house, ducking low to avoid the branches on the far perimeter.

As I mowed, I let my mind drift. My world had been turned upside down in less than a week. The strangeness had come with this intense, portentous heat, and there was no end in sight. First, Kennie had come back from hush-hush training the middle of last week, which I now knew had been her radical cheerleading camp. Then, at the planning meeting the next day, Dolly and Les interrupt the proceedings with their crazy talk about getting rid of Chief Wenonga. Lo and behold, the next morning the Chief disappeared and someone left behind a bloody chunk of head. That very day, an angry Gary Wohnt showed up at the library looking for me, a first.

Throw into that mix a missing Native American impersonator from yesterday's parade, and it all became too weird for words.

Dolly and Les were the most likely suspects, but I didn't like the smell of Brando Erikkson on the scene, especially since he was somehow connected to Les. I knew where those two were at the time the Indian mascot disappeared, though, so that put Dolly on the hook as suspect number one. I experienced a cheap thrill at the idea of pinning her as the culprit, but it was too easy. If you're going to steal two Native American representations, why announce your position at a very public meeting? If it were a publicity stunt, she would have claimed it by now—unless she had something else planned, like an Indian-stealing trifecta.

I returned to my other burning question: how does a twenty-three-foot statue disappear under the cover of night? I knew that the Battle Lake police officers trolled the main drag at least once every hour, so whoever took Chief Wenonga must be a pretty quick statue dismantler, which would point the finger squarely at Brando. But why would he steal the statue? He had a whole pile of 'em back in Wisconsin. It made more sense that Les, who made a name for himself flouting authority, would have removed the Chief. He certainly had access to the big equipment I would imagine was necessary—his brother owned a construction company in Perham.

Two hours of mowing, and I had a hot-sticky body but no answers. It wouldn't be easy, but I would have to find the Chief to find his abductor, and that's all there was to it. A good place to start would be to interview the people who lived in the handful of houses around Halvorson Park to see if they had seen or heard anything suspicious the night the Chief was stolen. That would be my next step. After that, I would visit Johnny's cabin, though the idea unsettled me. What game was he playing, asking me to watch his cabin, lying about leaving town immediately, and meeting up secretly with Dolly at the fireworks?

I parked the mower and walked on shaky legs back to the house. I considered taking another shower before I left but decided there was no point. Johnny had moved on. The Chief was gone. Who was I trying to impress? I hosed the grass flecks off my legs, turned the spray on the garden to refresh my vegetables, rinsed my face and hands in the chute of water, and hopped on my bike. The smell of gasoline lingered on me and became cloying in the concentrated heat of the midday sun, but I couldn't pedal fast enough to escape it. By the time I reached Halvorson Park, I was sweaty and flushed. The good news was that the 5K race was scheduled for today, so there were a lot of sweaty and flushed people around as well as a crowd to provide me cover.

When I strolled up to the house nearest to Halvorson, my bike at my side, I realized my luck was holding out. The tiny, 1950s square blue box of a house was having a garage sale. I parked my bike, sauntered up the driveway, and rummaged through a pile of old record albums, pausing to admire the bright cover of Engelbert Humperdinck's *After the Lovin'*. Next to me were two older ladies I didn't recognize.

"Isn't this your cookbook?" The white-haired woman nearest me held out a worn Doubleday Cookbook roughly the size of a wheelbarrow. She used a lot of her face when she talked.

"My name on the inside cover?"

The second white-haired woman opened it up. "Yup. Trudie Johannsen, 1952."

"Well, I'll be damned. I sold that at last year's all-town garage sale."

"You want it back?"

"How much is it?"

"Two dollars."

"Christ on a cracker! I can't hardly pass up a deal like that. Give it over."

The secret of the all-town garage sale was laid bare. Everyone was just recycling their stuff around town, year after year after year. I knew the high school was even selling old trophies they didn't have room for anymore.

I grabbed a frizzed-out hair tie with a nickel sticker on it and walked up to the scowling lady sitting at the card table, a steel box full of change in front of her. "Can I buy this hair tie?"

"If it's got a sticker on it, you can buy it."

I handed her a nickel and shoved the band into my pocket. "It must be weird not having Chief Wenonga to look at anymore." I gestured toward the park.

The woman glanced over at the Chief's former home, then back at me. She adjusted herself on the chair, one enormous polyester-clad thigh creating a sucking vacuum against the other. I noticed her eyebrows were overplucked and hung over each eye like a long gray toenail clipping. "You want to buy anything else?"

I looked around and reached for a half-full bottle of perfume next to her. "How much is this?"

"Fifty cents."

I gave her a dollar and waited for change. "I don't suppose you saw what happened?"

"Don't suppose. By the time I looked out, all there was to see was a girl standing there, her hands on the post." She jabbed her thumb in the general direction of where the Chief statue had been as she stared down into her change box. "Looked an awful lot like you."

I sucked in a quick little breath. "Really? Wouldn't that be hard to tell from this far away?"

"I got eyes like an eagle. You wouldn't want to buy that Vikings helmet, would you? Chris Carter wore it in 1996."

I looked at the beaten-up purple and gold football helmet and sighed. "How much?"

"Twenty dollars. Chris Carter wore it in 1996."

"Mmm hmm. There's a lot of women who look like me around, don't you think?"

"I think it depends on whether or not you want that helmet."

"Sold." I traded her a twenty for a helmet full of a stranger's sweat and high-tailed it out of there before she extorted any more cash out of me.

I didn't have any more luck at the next house over, or the next. At the fourth house I stopped at, I learned that the owner had seen a car leaving Halvorson Park early the morning the Chief disappeared. My heart soared until I was told the car was a small brown Toyota. Two people had seen either my car or me at the scene of the crime. Now I knew beyond a doubt why Gary Wohnt was after me.

Since no clues were forthcoming in this neighborhood, I hopped on my bike and pedaled out to Johnny's cabin, which was on Silver Lake, a mile and a half north and a little west of Halvorson Park. The lake was small and clean, but the west side was swamp so only the east side had cabins and houses on it. I had never been to Johnny's cabin, but last night at Stub's he had assured me that his name was on the mailbox, and there's only one way to go around a lake.

I pedaled the flat stretch to Silver Lake, coasting when I reached it so I could read the mailboxes. Sweat raced down between my shoulder blades, and I vowed to invest in some aluminum-laced, heavy-duty deodorant and anti-perspirant next time I was in the Apothecary. This sweltering heat wasn't gonna let up.

I pedaled the winding lake road once and didn't see Leeson printed on a mailbox. It was on the second pass that I noticed the dirt road snaking up into the woods to my left, at a spot where the tar road was veering away from the lake. I followed the dirt trail that led to a handful of tucked-away rustic cabins, so close together and similar that they looked almost like an abandoned resort. The cabin farthest from the entry road and closest to the lake had a black mailbox at the end of its driveway with "Leeson" painted in bronze on it.

I parked my bike and trod carefully toward the leaf-covered mud puddles in the center of the driveway. As I drew closer to the cabin, a hot breeze kicked through the treetops, making a scary whisper in the popple leaves. It was otherwise spooky quiet back here, except for the distant drone of an Evinrude. The other cabins must be summer retreats and looked unoccupied from where I stood. I stripped off my T-shirt and used it to wipe the sweat off my neck and chest, and, standing there in a sports bra and shorts, I wondered if it was a good idea to continue. No one knew where I was, and Battle Lake hadn't been a safe place as of late. I stood with my hands on my hips, T-shirt tucked in my waistband, and forced myself to get up some nerve. It was daylight, bright as a new penny, and nothing bad happened when the sun was out.

Seven long strides and I was at a low spot in the driveway. If it rained, this would be where the puddle would form. Right now, though, it didn't look like it had rained in this spot. It looked like a deer had been gutted and dressed out. There were brown winter leaves, probably carted in from the woods by Johnny, and they were smeared in crusty red. I grabbed a stick and poked at the pile until I dug up a white piece of rubber, stained red—one of the balloons, and when I pulled my stick back, it was also smeared with red. Whoever had driven over the balloons had done so within the last day. Judging by the amount of splatter, Johnny's plan had worked. The paint was still wet in spots. Whoever had been out here now had paint on their car.

I followed the faint red tire tracks leading toward the cabin, careful to keep to the clear, dry sections of road. My senses were hyper-tuned. I was sure that whatever kids had been out here messing around were gone, but I didn't know what they had left behind. The cabin itself looked small, maybe two big rooms inside, and the door must be facing the lake because I couldn't see it. The outside was covered in stained wood siding with a brown shake roof. It blended in nicely with the forest and was probably a great place to sneak a party if a person didn't know that Johnny was coming out here regularly.

I peered through the window closest to me, facing the driveway, and saw that there was in fact one big room inside, with a small kitchen, a bed, and steps to a loft. There was one door off the main room, and judging from the cabin's dimensions, it could only be a small bathroom. The bed looked rumpled and muddy.

More pressing, however, was the amount of light being let in through the wide open door on the lakeside of the cabin. Johnny had been right to worry. Some kids had broken in. I made my way around the building through the raspberry brambles, wondering why it was that people never did for themselves—landscapers had the messiest yards, chefs rarely ate at home, and carpenters' houses were never finished.

When I made it to the side of the cabin facing Silver Lake, the condition of the door startled me. It hung out, only one hinge left to secure it to the frame, and its lock and handle had been obliterated. Splinters of wood lay on the ground. I picked a chunk up, noting that it was quality wood, not the type I had in the double-wide. A pine scent laced with sawdust, mildew, and something disturbing that I couldn't quite place washed out of the cabin. The trespassing partiers had probably peed in a corner.

I wiped at the mosquitoes I had stirred up, and took a deep breath before going in. The inside of the cabin was surprisingly neat, except for the lumpy bed in the shadows. The central room was maybe twenty feet by twenty feet, and all the kitchen cupboards were closed and there were no dishes in the sink. I figured the smell must be coming from the bathroom, but when I pushed open the door, careful not to leave prints, only a simple toilet, cover up and water clean, and a pedestal sink stared back at me.

I sighed. The smell must be coming from the bed. I had avoided looking too closely at it because my fear was that Johnny's cabin bed had become the local lover's lane, and I didn't want to see that up close. I had come this far, though, and I might as well see her through. The rotten, coppery scent became overwhelming as I strode to the bed, and when I reached it, my brain didn't know what to make of the sight.

The sheets and blankets were rumpled like waves on the ocean, and pools of maroon so dark it was almost black marred their soft green surface. Was this more paint? I walked to the far side, where a nightstand stood between the bed and the wall. A blanket had fallen in this space. When I leaned in, I saw that the blanket was wearing a blood-crusted T-shirt, blue jeans, and one shoe. The other foot was bare and stiff from death, it's sheer whiteness the most disturbing sight. I couldn't look at the head, my eyes unable to let go of the image of that icy pale foot, sprinkled with wiry black hair on the toes and top.

I covered my nose, trying to stem the tide of nausea surfing on the musty smell of cabin and woods mixed with the heavy iron scent of violent death. The room fell sideways, and I caught myself from falling by lurching the other way. The buzzing in my ears made it impossible to think, and I stumbled out of the cabin, swallowing furiously to keep from throwing up. I could not leave any trace of me in this butcher shop.

Outside, I gulped in the fresh air of the forest, tears streaming down my face. Had Johnny and Dolly set me up?

SIXTEEN

I BIKED HOME IN a daze, showered, scrubbing my skin until it was raw, and drove to my pay phone of choice for making 911 calls. I called in the body at Johnny's cabin, giving the location but no details, not even my fake name. Afterward, I cruised to Gina's house, no longer caring if Wohnt saw me. She wasn't home, so I let myself in and helped myself to a glass of vodka on ice. That had been my dad's favorite drink, minus the ice. I could see where a person could get used to it. The slightly antiseptic taste felt good going down, disinfecting your memories and blotting out dark thoughts.

By my second glass of vodka, I was beginning to feel in control again. So what if Johnny and Dolly had killed a guy, hid the corpse in his cabin, and set me up to take the fall? I had outsmarted them. No one knew I had been to the cabin, and now, the police were going to find the body and nail those two. You couldn't really blame them for choosing me as their patsy, anyhow. Finding dead bodies had so far been one of my recurring occupations in Battle

Lake, so I had good references. And what did I care? I didn't need anybody. I was just fine being alone. You don't get hurt if you're alone.

I dozed off for a while and was awakened by the fierce growl of my stomach. Now that I had my life in order, going to the Fortune Café for a late lunch seemed like a grand idea. I stumbled out the door, wondering when it had gotten so damn hot outside. Certain that my car ignition had turned into the bake switch on an oven, I decided to walk. I had traipsed almost to the front door of the café when I felt an ominous presence loom behind me, blocking out the sweltering July sun. I turned to see a steely-eyed Gary Wohnt staring me down.

"I've been looking for you."

I swayed slightly, then fixed him with an icy stare. I had to squint one eye a little to do it. "Gary."

"Where are you going?"

Answer nothing, deny everything, make counter accusations. "Where are *you* going?"

"I need you to come to the station to answer some questions, Ms. James."

"OK, well I'm free later this afternoon, maybe around 4:00?"

"Now."

"Can't we just talk here?"

"I don't think you want that."

"Fine." I tossed my head with what I hoped was arrogant innocence, but to tell the truth, I felt a little green around the gills. Gary Wohnt and I silently walked the two blocks to the Battle Lake Police Station. The three-room brick building was stifling. The open windows allowed in the pizza-oven hot air of the late morning, and the lazy ceiling fan circulated it down into my face.

"Why don't you have a seat, Ms. James." It was not a question.

I pulled up the metal chair with a screech and sat down so I was facing Gary Wohnt across his desk. I was going to outlast him. He had nothing on me. I would stare him down, one mask of control to another. We might be here for days, but I would not talk.

"I didn't take Wenonga. I was only there on Friday morning because I noticed he was gone. I was going to tell you but I was worried you'd think I had something to do with stealing him. I wouldn't steal him. I loved him. Those were my fingerprints on the one post, but that was just an accident." *Dammit.*

Wohnt sighed and closed his eyes for ten long seconds, his fingers forming a teepee over the bridge of his nose. "That's not why I asked you to come here today, Ms. James. You are here because two hours ago, a dead body was found in Jonathan Leeson's cabin on Silver Lake, and you were the last confirmed person seen in Mr. Leeson's company."

Shit. He was up to date. "Why aren't you out there now?"

"There are officers on the scene. In fact, the FBI has been called in. I would like to be able to present as much information as possible to them when they arrive. You can help me with that." He leaned back in his chair, but his posture did not give an inch. "Do you know where Mr. Leeson is right now?"

I knew where he told me he was going to be. Visiting his grandma in Stevens Point. However, I was very sure that was not where he was. "Did you ask his mom?"

"Mrs. Leeson said she believed her son was staying at the cabin for the night and does not know his current whereabouts."

"Do you know whose body it is?"

"We haven't positively identified the body. What did you and Mr. Leeson visit about at Stub's last night?"

"Ummm, gardening mostly."

"Are you dating Mr. Leeson?"

I snorted involuntarily. "No."

"I think it'd be best if you submitted a set of your fingerprints."

"Right now?"

"Yes."

"Do I have to?"

"We would look favorably upon it if you did."

"Do I have to?"

"I highly recommend it."

"Do I have to?"

"No."

I took a deep breath. "Then I think I'll go. OK?"

"Don't go far."

I was walking toward the door, worried that Wohnt was going to change his mind about letting me go but unable to stop the question leaking out my mouth. "The body you found. Was it missing part of its scalp?"

Gary Wohnt had closed his eyes again, so I couldn't tell what he was thinking, but for a second, it sounded like there was humor in his voice. "Yes. It was."

As I pushed outside into the hairy wall of heat, my head was reeling, and it didn't stop until I entered the door of the Fortune Café. The cool air laced with ginger and chocolate brought my anxiety down a notch. I would get to the bottom of this. The whole Battle Lake world was in a steaming latrine, and I needed to fix it. Not to save anyone else, mind you, but for my own peace of mind and so the cops would leave me alone. I'd find the Chief, and Bill Myers, and discover why Dolly and Johnny had hidden a body in his cabin for me to find. Those who had messed up would pay. I squared my shoulders and walked up to the counter and directly into the lusty path of Brando Erikkson's gaze. He stood from his two-chair table and strode toward me.

"Mira! Two run-ins in under twenty-four hours. Fate must be bringing us together."

"It's a small town," I grumbled. "It's gravity bringing us together."

"Ha ha! Will you join me?"

I looked around the tiny café, dominated by a large glass display case leading to the kitchens in back. It was lunch rush, and there were no empty tables. I poked my head around the corner to the game room and library and still saw no place to sit. I considered getting some coffee to go, but reminded myself of my newfound commitment to get to the bottom of things. That included talking to Brando to find out what he knew. I might as well do it in public, in the daylight. "Sure."

I started to walk toward the counter, but Brando put his arm on mine. "I'll get it. What would you like?"

I sat down reluctantly. "An iced coffee and a cinnamon scone would be fine, thank you." I grudgingly admired his very tight rear as he walked toward the counter. Too bad he gave me the creeps. My brain stayed quiet until he returned.

"Here you go."

"Thanks."

Brando set the coffee and scone in front of me, but instead of sitting at the chair across the table, he stood, leaning into it. "You didn't come to my party last night."

I sipped the sweet, cool coffee and felt it slice through some of the fog on my brain. "I was tired. I went home."

"Too bad. It was a great time. Good music, good drinks, hot men." He winked at me, and stretched his hands over his head like a cat in a sunbeam.

"Great."

"Yes, this is a nice little town you have here. The woodchuck is going to fit in real nice."

I coughed on a piece of scone. "I was going to ask you about that. Why a woodchuck?"

Brando smirked and ran a hand sinuously up his own thigh and stroked his chest through his shirt. He placed one foot on his chair, giving me a full view of his testicle cleavage. I was pretty sure he was about ready to ask me to cup his balls when I realized what he was doing. He was flirting with himself, with me as his audience.

"Can you please sit down? It's hard to talk to you when you're standing."

Brando looked slightly taken aback, and then disappointed, but he plunked down. "You're a feisty one."

"Not so much. Bitter is probably a better word. So why the woodchuck? Why not another Chief Wenonga?"

He ran his fingers through his glossy black hair. "Indian chiefs are costly to make. It takes weeks to make any of the big men, but the Indians take even longer. We start out with a single statue mold for all of them, and from that, we create any variety of roadside art—Paul Bunyans, Muffler Men, Carolina Cowboy, Jesus Christ. For those guys, we just place different objects in the hands, like axes or crosses, but for the Indian line, we needed to build a whole new chest and arms for the mold. We don't even make them anymore. In fact, we only made three statues out of that Chief Wenonga mold."

"You're in a weird line of work."

Brando shook his head in disagreement, donning his salesman cap. "Not at all! My dad started out making boats in Wisconsin, but we needed something to do during the off-season, so we started making the big men. The work was crude at first, but now it's art. I don't sell anything that isn't absolutely perfect."

"Which is why you're giving away the woodchuck?"

"It's face melted a little. You can hardly tell when you're driving past it."

"When is Battle Lake getting the woodchuck?"

"It's on its way as we speak, from Stevens Point, Wisconsin."

Click. Last night Johnny told me he was visiting his grandma in Stevens Point. Brando's company is in Stevens Point. Too much coincidence. "You know Johnny Leeson?"

"Oh yeah, he's that albino guy in that band. The one with the brother. I like their stuff." Brando took this opportunity to slide his hand across the table and onto my arm. I grabbed my coffee and brought it to my lips, slurping the last of it and wrenching my arm out of reach.

"Not Johnny Winter. Johnny Leeson. He's from Battle Lake."

"Never heard of him."

I got the distinct impression Brando didn't pay much attention to men. "So how long does it take to dismantle a statue like Chief Wenonga?"

Brando's eyes flashed sharply, so quickly that I might have imagined it, and then went back to their half-lidded state. "I don't know. I'm an artist, not a construction worker. That was before my modeling career, you know."

If his reference to modeling was meant to impress me, it was a wasted effort. "If you make the statues, you have to have some idea of how they come apart."

He sighed and leaned back heavily in his chair, looking bored. "You only have one-note women in this town? That Kennie Rogers is about as interesting as hemorrhoid surgery, too. Sloppy kisser, by the way."

I clenched my fists. I wasn't going to sign up for Kennie's fan club anytime soon, but knocking her was my job, not his. "You can say a lot of things about Kennie, but the woman is not boring. And the only thing worse than a sloppy kisser is a man who kisses and tells. So what do you know about taking fiberglass statues apart?"

He looked at me out of the corner of his eyes, still pouting. "Like I said, the statues are made from fiberglass in open molds. Then we bond the seams together, and you've got a statue. We set them up; we don't take them down."

The bell on the front door twinkled, and Brittany and Heaven strolled in. Brando's eyes were on them like metal on a magnet, and I was immediately invisible.

"Never? You never take them down?"

"Huh?"

Brittany and Heaven sauntered to the front and bent over the baked goods display case, their Daisy Dukes magically covering their lower ass shelf. Or maybe they didn't have lower ass shelves. Suddenly angry myself, I grabbed my empty plate and glass and set them on the bus cart behind me. I flicked Brando on his head to get his attention. "You've *never* taken a statue down?"

He kept his gaze on the eye candy, a sneer on his well-formed lips. "No. You'd need a wrecking ball for that. There's no way to take one of those statues down without destroying it."

SEVENTEEN

Ouch. Until now, I had assumed that Chief Wenonga had been statue-napped and was in a warehouse somewhere, or maybe an empty silo, whole and perhaps missing me. Brando Erikkson's careless words were crushing that dream. I needed to face facts: Chief Wenonga was gone, never to return. I tried that reality on for size for thirty whole seconds, staring at the side of Brando's head as he stared at Brittany and Heaven's behinds. "You're a dumb ass," I said, and whisked myself out. My made-from-scratch reality was going to win this one.

Underneath my bravado, however, I was hurting. I needed to clear my head, and that meant a whole afternoon of gardening. The fates had a different plan for me, unfortunately.

"Mira! Mira James! Just the girl we need." Kennie strolled over to me as I left the Fortune. I stared, confused, at the crowd with her. "Gary Wohnt was supposed to help me judge the pets and owners look-alike contest, but he just got called away. You can fill in for him and write a neat little article for the *Recall* while you're at it."

I shook my head so vehemently that something wobbled loose. "No. Absolutely not. I have plans."

"Twenty minutes, that's all we need," Kennie sang, smiling down at me from the teetering heights of her four-inch espadrilles.

"What about all these people with you?" I gestured at the hopeful-looking crowd behind her.

"Friends and family of the pet owners, and therefore not eligible to judge. Come along. Twenty minutes, I cross my heart and hope to cry. And phoo-ee, do you smell ripe. I'm gonna have to come over later and do you a favor."

That sentence was so ominous that my mouth clicked shut until Kennie dragged me to the spot where the turtle races were usually held. The crowd followed along, apparently relieved that their loved ones were going to get a chance to be judged for how much they looked like animals. Kennie shoved a pad in my hands.

"You and me need to agree on a score between one and ten, with ten being the most resemblance."

"Fine. Let's get it done and over with." There were only ten names on the pad. According to the pad, six of them were dog owners, one owned a ferret, one owned a fish, and two owned cats.

We walked past the contestants, both animals and owners drooping in the afternoon heat. Kennie cooed at how cute the pets were and I wondered whether people chose animals who looked like them, or whether we all just started looking like our pets after awhile. If so, I was hoping for some Tiger Pop highlights.

"Well, aren't you just the sweetest!" Kennie had stopped next to a fat Golden Retriever whose name on the pad was listed as "Kasey." Next to Kasey was a fat blonde man with friendly bags under his eyes. When the dog blinked, he blinked. The two even had matching jowls. Kennie and I looked at each other and both wrote down a ten.

Next was a man and his five-inch Blue Gill on a stringer. "Curtis Poling!" It was the first good news I'd had all day. Curtis Poling was a charming and slightly bawdy man who lived in the Senior Sunset, a few rooms down from Mrs. Berns. He fished off the roof, so people said he was crazy, but I knew that he was crazy like a fox and twice as cute. He had helped me crack Jeff's murder in May. "What're you doing out?"

"I wanted to see about getting my fish mounted, but somehow, I ended up over here. She's a beaut, eh?"

The fish was big for a sunny, and it was stinky. "Catch her off the roof?"

Curtis winked at me. "You know it. If you got a spot that works, you stick with it."

"You know, you don't look anything like that fish, Curtis."

"And neither do you, darling. I'd thank you to head me back toward the taxidermy shop, and I'll be on my way." His smile crinkled his ice-blue eyes, still sharp as hooks even though Curtis was pushing ninety.

"You got it, Curtis. Just let me finish up." Kennie had moved on quickly when she saw the dead fish, and when I caught up with her, we agreed that Kasey the retriever and her owner Bill were the winners. For their efforts, they received a $25 gift certificate to Scooby's Doo, the local pet grooming parlor. I thanked everyone for participating, took Curtis by the elbow, and led him back to the Sunset, making a quick detour to the taxidermy shop on our way.

Once I knew Curtis was safe at the Sunset, I went back to Gina's house to retrieve my car and headed home, forcibly keeping negative thoughts out of my head. That left me idea-free, and it occurred to me with wicked irony that I now knew what it was like to be a Brittany. The lush hardwoods along County Road 83 looked tropical, but there were still no birds singing. The silence made the heat pregnant, and I wondered when it was going to break. I added "swim in the lake" to my mental list of cleansing activities for this afternoon.

At least my animals were happy to see me, Luna pumping happily up the driveway. Back at the house, I promised ice water and a cool dip in the lake if she'd let me get into my swimsuit and slap on some sunscreen. Tiger Pop had feigned disinterest in lapping up ice water and swimming, but he followed us as we made our way down the tree-shaded lane to our tiny little private beach on Whiskey Lake. I could hear families splashing at Shangri-La, the charming resort at the end of the isthmus that was the wide spot at this end of my driveway.

I tossed my towel to the ground and kept to the grass, avoiding the pile of brown sugar sand the local 4H club had delivered this summer. The sand, I knew from painful experience, would be glass-making hot this time of day. Sunlight shimmered bright off the smooth surface of the lake, so bright I couldn't look straight at it. Head down, I walked into the heavenly cool water until I was knee deep and took the plunge. I was never one to acclimate myself slowly. I twisted underwater, my body heat sinking agreeably.

My hands played along the silty bottom of the lake and dragged through the plant life. If I had on my diving mask, I'd be able to see silvery fish dart away from my intrusion. As I swam, the image of that dead white foot in Johnny's cabin kept sliding into my brain, and it left a cold, empty feeling inside of me. Suddenly, I didn't feel like being in this big lonely lake anymore.

I pushed myself to the surface, and Luna whined at me from the shore.

"Come on, you big baby!"

She barked, once, and paddled out to me. I knew she'd scratch me if she got too close, so I avoided her as I stroked back in. I found a piece of driftwood and played fetch with her in two feet of water. When she was exhausted and the cool water at my feet had leeched the red from my face, I headed back to the house, not bothering to towel off. Luna and Tiger Pop trailed behind, my sweet little farm groupies.

The part of the garden I hadn't worked over on Friday night had reached the Extreme Weeding stage. The plants were Land-of-the-Lost massive, and the weeds had stopped seeding weeks ago. If I gave it a good going-over today and used the dead weeds as mulch, I would only have to do occasional, light weeding for the rest of the summer. Fortunately, that section was in the shade at this time of day.

I picked up where I had left off and dug my fingers into the earth, enjoying the cool feel under the surface. I started at the outer perimeter of the broccoli, cauliflower, and Brussels sprout cans. By the time I got to the peas, my rhythm was down to a science. I didn't even stop to snack on the juicy pods. Next it was carrots, then beans, eggplant, squash, and pumpkins, and finally, more marigolds and zinnias. I knew I'd be flush with zinnias by the first blush of August. By the time I was on the final row, the weeds I'd laid flat at the first were turning a dried, lightening green, serving as a warning for all future trespassers. It would also keep the roots of my vegetables cooler during the scorching July days. For good measure, I raked up two piles of drying grass from my earlier lawn-mowing and scattered an extra layer of mulch over the weeds.

When finished, hands on my hips, crusty dirt caked to my knees and under my fingernails, I studied my work. The garden was lush and organized, and looked like a clean straw bed. Food and comfort, in one small, thriving space. I stretched and studied the position of the sun, figuring it was about 10:30. I decided to check the bird-seed level in my feeders and set out the sprinkler to wet the thirsty earth in my garden, and then go inside to make supper. I was leaning into the five-gallon metal birdseed bucket when I heard a car coming up my driveway. I figured it was just some guest heading to Shangri-La and continued my work. I had a big scoop of seed in hand when the car pulled into my driveway. My stomach clenched when I realized the car belonged to Kennie Rogers. It dropped down to my knees when I saw who was in the seat next to her.

EIGHTEEN

"Aren't we lucky to catch you at home, Miss Mira!"

I was frozen, gripping a scoop of thistle seed like it was the key to The Door Out. Kennie had warned me that she was coming over later, and what a fool I was for not believing her.

"Brad, I do declare, we are just in time for a Beaver Pelt intervention, wouldn't you say? If ever a girl needed to feel pretty, that girl was Mira." Kennie strode over to me purposefully, the white lab coat she was wearing over knee-high pleather go-go boots doing nothing to relax my stance.

Bad Brad, the man I once thought I loved until he had cheated on me, thank God, was still in Battle Lake after his Friday night concert. Worse, he was at Kennie's side, a snap-front lab coat with a skull and crossbones pattern covering him head to shorts. He wore scruffy Doc Marten boots and had what looked like a doctor's house-call bag in hand. I might have whimpered.

"Now, don't look so scared. My assistant and I are here to save you, if you're ready to be saved."

For sure I wasn't. I dropped the scoop into the metal bucket and started backing toward the house. It was a flimsy double-wide so this little pig didn't have much protection, but my only other option was my car, and Drs. Moreau and Hyde were between me and it. "Saved sounds great! Let me just go get cleaned up real quick, and we can get on with that."

Brad and Kennie continued advancing, smiling encouragingly. "But that's why we're here. To clean you up, doll!"

My plan was to get inside the double-wide, lock the front door, and while they tried to break in and have their most certainly unlicensed "Beaver Pelt intervention" way with me, I would slip out the back window and into my car. And then, I would drive as far away from Battle Lake as I could humanly get on one tank of gas while wearing a bikini. "Can I wash my hands?"

"No need, sweetie. We have gloves, and we do all the handling. You just lay there!"

I squealed and tripped over my own feet, landing on the soft grass in an ungainly heap. Brad leaned down and offered me his hand. "Jeez, Mira. It's no big deal. Kennie is just running a home visit cosmopologist service."

"Cosmetologist, hon', but my specialty is waxing. Eyebrows, mustaches, down below. I got the inspiration from the Beaver Pelts cheerleading squad. Those short skirts, all those old legs in the air. That's where I got the name, of course—Beaver Pelt Intervention. It's a waist to big toe waxing, all for one low price."

I blinked, noisily, and got to my feet without the help of Brad. "You came here to give me a bikini wax? With Brad?"

"I assure you I'm licensed. It's been a decade or so since I took the classes at Alex Tech, but I've kept current through a correspondence program."

"And Brad? What're you doing here?" I was suddenly self-conscious in my two-piece swimsuit and drew my thighs together in a slow and controlled movement, so as not to draw attention to my "down below."

Brad smiled serenely. "I have you to thank for that, Mira. I was going to go back with the band Friday after I saw you, but dude, you just looked so happy. I wanted to see if the small town life would work for me, too, especially since I had a connection with you here already. When Kennie came by to pay us Friday night, she said I could crash at her place until I could get myself settled."

Kennie looked from Brad to me, a cross between crabby and curious. "You two know each other?"

"Not anymore," I said.

"And not like I know you, right, hon?" Kennie winked at Brad.

I suddenly noticed Brad's legs were hairless. I turned off my brain before the picture went any farther north, but damn if karma wasn't dealing me a confusing hand. My cheating ex was in town, but he appeared to be facing his own punishment at the hand of a crazy waxer. I couldn't process it. What I needed was a shower, supper, and a little bland television. "I appreciate you driving out here, Kennie, but I don't get waxed."

"There's a first time for everything."

"Not true."

"I'll give you a 50 percent discount."

"Kennie, I'm not going to pay you to rip my hair out with hot wax."

"I'm not leaving until I help you out, sweets. How about a teeny tiny little makeover?" She raised her penciled-in eyebrows hopefully.

"How teeny tiny?"

"Just a little mascara and a dust of lip gloss. It'll brighten your pretty eyes right up. They're all deep set now, like holes in your skull."

I sighed. Kennie clearly was not going to leave until she touched me, so my face seemed like the safest bet. I wasn't going to let them in my house, though. I rinsed off as best I could with the garden hose and set myself on the front porch steps, hands on knees. Brad opened up his doctor's bag to reveal a pot of wax, strips of paper, an evil-looking four-inch tweezers, a comb, brush, scissors, hairspray, and a full palette makeup kit. He pulled out the latter and held it open for Kennie, who studied me disapprovingly.

"You're tanned as brown as a bean farmer."

"Sorry."

"You're going to look like raisin leather before you're forty, you know that? And you have fieldworker hands."

"Just do the makeup, okay? I haven't had supper yet."

Kennie sniffed and huffed but didn't say anything else as she began applying makeup. This close to her face, I could see the putty-knife precision she used to get herself through the day. There was a bronze makeup lip around the perimeter of her face, and her purple, blue, and pink eye shadow was thick and unblended. Her lips were clownish, as if drawn by a four-year-old. Sigh. At least I was home, and I could wash off whatever damage she did.

Brad tried to make supportive "ooh-ing" sounds throughout the process, but his eyes kept getting wider and wider as I felt myself buried under Kennie's fall colors. Even Luna and Tiger Pop were watching now.

Twenty long minutes later, Kennie pronounced herself done. "That is what they call a make*over*. Brad, hand me the mirror."

I thought of the "Mira Mira" song Brad had sung to me on Friday. "No—Mira. I mean, mirror," I said. "I'm sure it looks fabulous. How much do I owe you?"

Kennie chuckled. "Honey, consider me your drug dealer. The first one is free, and once I get you hooked, we talk prices. Now don't waste that pretty face at home. You'all should come to town tonight and show yourself off."

I smiled at the unlikeliness of that happening. "Good idea. I suppose you two need to go drum up more business, eh?"

"You know the life of the working woman too well! Never rest for the wicked. You know where to find me." She twittered her fingers at me and herded Brad away before he had fully closed his doctor's bag. I was not sorry to see them go. I made a mental note to start carrying my stun gun around with me, even if I was wearing a bikini. I went inside to wash my face off in a cool shower. I was locking the door behind me—I hadn't totally ruled out Kennie resorting to a forcible bikini wax—when the phone rang. I didn't bother to check the caller ID.

"Hello?"

"Mira? It's Johnny."

My heart thudded on a crest of mixed feelings. "Where are you?"

"I'm still in Stevens Point. In Wisconsin."

My voice took on an edge. "And how's your grandma?"

I heard a deep sigh through the crackling of the phone line. Johnny must be calling on his cell. "I'm sorry, Mira. I never went to see my grandma. I lied to you."

More confusion. "Why?"

"I needed you to watch my cabin, and if I told you where I was really going, I didn't know if you'd do it."

"So where did you really go?"

There was another crackle on the line. "...Stevens Point. Dolly teaches here, at the University of..."

He faded out, but I had heard enough. I almost hung up when his voice ghosted back over the line. "She vandalized a McDonald's."

"What? You were cutting out."

"Hold on." There was a little more static, and then his voice came through like a crystal. "I came to Stevens Point to find out what I could about Dolly Castle. Last night when you saw us at the fireworks? I was trying to find out where she teaches. I think she's behind the disappearance of Chief Wenonga, and I wanted to go to where she works and lives to see what I could find out."

My heart warmed a crack. Was it possible Johnny was just as interested in getting the Chief back as I was, and really had a legitimate reason to lie and hang out with Dolly? "And you found out she vandalized a McDonald's?"

"Not the building, the Ronald McDonald statues out front. A whole chain of them in India. Apparently, she was over there for study abroad in some place called Shatrunjaya Hills, and her group went activist and spray painted messages on the Ronald McDonalds, cut off limbs, added horns. Dolly was arrested and extradited to the United States. She ended up paying a hefty fine."

"So what does that tell us?"

"I don't know. That she knows how to mess with fiberglass? That she's not afraid of breaking the law? You sound mad. I thought you would think this was good news."

My thawing heart ached. Johnny really did sound like he wanted to impress me. The one important point he had failed to address was the dead body in the cabin he had asked me to watch for him. "Is there anything else you called about?"

"…can't hear you…"

"IS THERE ANYTHING ELSE YOU WANT TO TELL ME?"

"…reception…of nowhere…"

"THERE IS A DEAD BODY IN YOUR CABIN. DO YOU WANT TO TALK ABOUT IT?"

"…body in my dad's cabin? What are you talking about?"

I lowered my voice to normal range. "The police found a dead body in your cabin today. Now they're looking for you. Whose body is it?" The other end of the line was absolutely quiet. "Johnny? Whose body is it?"

His voice came out hushed, and it wasn't the connection. "I have no idea, Mira."

Tears stung my eyes. "Don't lie to me. Please don't lie to me."

"I have no idea whose body it is. I'm on my way back. I'll go straight to the police station and…"

There was a snap on the line, and it went dead. I held it to my ear for several seconds longer, and then hit the "end" button on my phone. My caller ID registered only an "Unknown Name, Unknown Number" for the call. I sat tensely on my couch, wishing I had brought Gina's bottle of vodka home with me.

NINETEEN

I SQUARED MY SHOULDERS. As much as I wanted to believe Johnny knew nothing about the dead guy, I was not going to let myself be played the fool again. I tried to shove pictures of Johnny out of my head, but in the sultry heat of my living room, I couldn't escape the images of him smiling at me as he helped me landscape in June, ignoring the bruises discoloring my face, or the image of his strong hands digging into black dirt, or even the picture of his sweetly shy smile as he dropped me off after supper last night. These hot thoughts pulsed through my mind as a mosquito whined around my head. I slapped at it and missed, and it was soon joined by a second.

I checked my front door, and it was locked tight. I couldn't find a hole in any of the screens, either. I fixed myself a cold cheese and pickle sandwich and scarfed it down. I rinsed the plate, stacked it in the sink, and made myself a glass of ice water. The glass fogged up immediately, and drips of water glided down the sides and over my fingers. By now more mosquitoes had joined the first ones, their telltale humming promising a miserable night.

I tried to outrun them by dashing into my bedroom and slamming the door. I set the sweating water glass next to my bed and flopped down, a fan pointed on my body. I wanted to think, but whenever the breeze from the oscillating fan moved from my head, the mosquitoes returned, buzzing and keening with a vengeance. It sounded like a bona fide swarm, but I couldn't seem to kill them. When I pointed the fan so it was aimed only at my face, one of them bit my ankle and escaped scot-free.

Frustrated, I tried lying under the sheets to escape the mosquitoes, but I could still hear their vibrations. They were hovering, just waiting for me to relax and expose my soft and vulnerable skin. I tossed and turned and wondered what Gary Wohnt would do to Johnny. Throw him into the county jail in Fergus Falls, certainly, and how would they treat him there? He was too pretty to be in jail. I was bitten again, this time on the tender flesh of my wrist, and I jumped out of bed and returned to the couch. The whine of the mosquitoes was driving me crazy. I couldn't think a clear thought and I certainly couldn't sleep between the heavy heat and the bloodthirsty flying knives invading my home. My choices were either to stay here and go insane, or go into town and see if the Battle Lake Motel had a vacancy. I could fix whatever chink in my double-wide armor they were coming through tomorrow, in the light of day.

Before I started to fret about the money I'd be wasting, I scooped up a toothbrush, change of clothes, and a hairbrush and headed out the door. I made sure to let Tiger Pop and Luna out to spend the night in the hay-filled barn, where they would be much cooler and where they had fresh water. I could still hear the whining insects as I got in my car, so I rolled down all the windows and sped down County Road 83. Only when I finally reached the outskirts of Battle Lake did I feel bug-free.

When I pulled into the motel parking lot, I spotted Dolly's black Honda and, a few cars down, Brando's red Humvee. When I had questioned him at his shop after the parade Indian disappeared, Les had said Brando was staying in a cabin north of town, but I had no reason to trust him. Brando could be staying at the motel, for all I knew, or maybe he was visiting Dolly, confirming my earlier hunch. Was the motel his destination when he tailgated me a couple days earlier, on the day I had discovered the missing Chief?

A little window peeking was clearly in order, but first, I was going to stop by and visit Chief Wenonga's post to see if there was anything I had missed when I had first found the scalp. Heat lightning flashed across the glass-flat surface of Battle Lake as I stepped out of my car, and it gave me chills. A storm in this heat would be fierce. I sniffed the air for ozone but only smelled lake and country. I reached back into my car for my flashlight and headed to Wenonga's former home. The half-full moon offered enough illumination that I didn't click on my light as I walked, listening to the tinkle of glasses and muted laughter floating across the lake.

The base was just as I had left it, two days and a million years ago, minus the blood. The four posts had been scrubbed clean and pointed angrily toward the night sky. They were cool to the touch, as was the four-foot-high cement stand. Clicking on my flashlight revealed nothing new on the stand, and the grass perimeter was also scrubbed clean—not even a cigarette butt marred the trampled

145

grass. That gave me pause. Footprints were the only thing that had been around Chief Wenonga's base on Friday when I discovered him missing, as well. If the Chief-stealer had used a wrecking ball, as Brando had said they would have had to, there would have been Chief shrapnel everywhere. Instead, the ground had been as clean as a hospital floor.

I got on my knees and ran my fingers through the stubbly grass to make sure I wasn't missing something.

"What're you doing?"

The gruff voice made me jump up so quickly that I lost my flashlight. I couldn't make out anyone in the light of the half-moon. "Who said that?"

"I am the night. I am swift justice. I am—"

"Les, is that you?"

He shuffled out from behind a tree, a set of night-vision goggles perched on his head. I reached down for my flashlight, sending a crazy strip of light down the park, and shined it on Les. He was dressed head to toe in Realtree camo with black mud or grease paint smeared across his cheeks.

"What're you doing out here late at night?"

"I could ask you the same thing, Les."

"I'm hunting."

"For what?"

"The truth."

"I guess I am, too. You find any?"

"Not yet, but I just started." The front office door to the Battle Lake Motel opened, spilling a rectangle of yellow light out into the parking lot. Les hit the ground and pulled me with him. "Get down!"

I had no choice but to hit the grass next to Les. "You wouldn't happen to be searching for this truth at the Battle Lake Motel, would you be?"

"Perhaps."

A thought struck me. "You know where Brando is staying?"

"I already told you. A cabin north of town."

"So what's his Humvee doing at the motel?"

Les broke off eye contact with me. The motel door closed and we both stood up, brushing the dirt off our knees.

"Les?"

"Could be he's visiting someone."

I decided to come at this from behind. "Say, Les, how would you take down the Chief Wenonga statue if you had to do it?"

He eyed me suspiciously. "I didn't steal the statue."

I sighed. "Look, I saw you following Dolly at the fireworks, and now you're spying on her outside her motel room. If I tell Gary Wohnt what you're up to, you're going to have an uncomfortable lot of surveillance in your life. How about you cooperate with me now, and I'll keep quiet about your illicit activities?"

He started to puff up, his bowling-ball face glistening under the blackness, and then, just as quickly, he deflated. "I'm just guessing, you understand? I didn't take that statue, but if I did, I'd take it down with a blowtorch and a cherry picker, lickety split. No mess, and you could get it done in under forty-five minutes. That's just a guess, mind you."

I processed that and wondered why Brando had lied. Or maybe he really had no idea how to dismantle a fiberglass statue? "What were you talking to Brando about the other night, when he stormed out of your store?"

147

Les shuffled his feet in the dirt. "I knew he was coming to town. I overheard Kennie and Gary talking about it one night when I was strolling past Kennie's house. I arranged a visit with Brando, thinking I could talk him into making a big white guy statue for the town."

I'll bet he was just strolling past Kennie's house. I wonder who else's house he strolled past regularly. "What did Brando say?"

"He didn't think it would be a good idea. Say, you look awful pretty tonight."

The incongruousness of his statement made it hard to process. "What?"

Another door opened in the Battle Lake Motel, but this time, it wasn't the office door. It was door number 7—Dolly Castle's door—and a victorious-looking Brando was emerging. Both Les and I dropped to the ground automatically, and I had to stifle a yelp when Dolly's strawberry blonde head peeked out and kissed Brando passionately before slapping him on the rear and closing the door behind him. They did know each other.

"How do Brando and Dolly know each other?" I looked away from the rumbling Humvee. "Les?" He was gone, like a mole underground. I sighed and stood, dragging my exhausted bones back to the motel. I needed some sleep so I could mull over everything I had seen and heard today, from the dead body at the cabin to the tryst I had just witnessed.

I entered the motel office and dinged the bell at the front desk. I heard a cheerful voice warble from the back room. "I'm on my way! It's a busy night here at the Battle Lake Motel. We have just one...oh my!"

The face of the middle-aged desk clerk went from welcoming to surprised to suspicious. I looked over my shoulder—no one there—and back at her, smiling uncertainly. "Um, were you saying you have one room left?"

"We're a family hotel."

"Oh, it's just me tonight."

"We are a family motel." Her lips pursed into an uptight moue. "We don't need your kind's business."

I looked around the front office, trying to find some indication of what my kind was versus what kind they were accepting. That's when I caught my reflection off the glass of the 5 by 7 framed Ducks Unlimited print over the front desk. My face still wore all the makeup that Kennie had put on me earlier, and it did not look pretty, unless one was in the market for a ten-dollar whore. "Jesus."

"It's a little late for him, don't you think?"

"No, I mean yes! I mean, I'm not what you think I am. I, um, let my five-year-old niece put makeup on my face earlier tonight and must have forgotten to wash it off. My name is Mira James. I run the library and work at the newspaper."

Her lips stayed as tight as a razor cut across her face. "And why do you need a hotel room if you live in town, Ms. James?"

"I don't live in town. I live west of town, in Sunny Waters' double-wide?" I knew I was going a little crazy from stress because I hardly ever referred to the double-wide as Sunny's anymore. "There's a hole in one of the screens, but I can't find where, and the place is swarming with mosquitoes. I needed to get a good night's sleep. OK?"

Her lips relaxed only marginally. "I need to see some ID."

Thankfully, my new driver's license had arrived in the mail the week before. Heaven help me if I handed her something with a Minneapolis address. I pulled out my driver's license and handed it over. "See? I live west of town."

She snapped the plastic card on the counter and slid it toward me. "I hope I don't see any male companionship entering your room tonight, Ms. James. It would be a shame if I had to call Battle Lake Police Chief Gary Wohnt out here to interrupt your, ahem, activities."

"I'm pretty sure you don't have to worry about me receiving any male companionship in the near future. How much is the room?"

"$55 plus tax. Because it's still a holiday weekend."

"Gotcha." I handed her my cash and took my room key. Lucky number 8, right next to Dolly, who was doing just fine for male companionship, thank you very much. I bet she hadn't gotten the hairy eyeball from the desk clerk.

I grabbed the small bundle of toiletries from my car and headed toward my room, grateful at the prospect of a night in air-conditioned comfort. There was one last hunch I needed to follow up on before I retired for the night, though.

I stopped at Dolly's car, my flashlight in my hands, and dropped to my knees. In the moonlight, I didn't see anything but gravel clumps, but when I ran my hands over the bumps and they didn't come off, I shined my light and peered closer. Sure enough—there was dried red paint mixed amid the dirt. It looked like Dolly had done a little four-wheeling out at Johnny's cabin, and recently.

TWENTY

I slept well in the air-conditioned motel and woke up feeling like I could solve all this and bring Chief Wenonga home to Battle Lake. After seeing Brando leave Dolly's room, and then finding the red paint on Dolly's car, it was plain as the mosquito bites on my ankle that Dolly and Brando were my bad guys. I just had to figure out how and why. After I showered and got the library up and running, I would go out to Johnny's cabin to see if I had missed anything, and then I'd enlist Gary Wohnt's help to get Johnny off the hook. Together, we'd find out why the Chief had been taken, how it was connected to the disappearance of Bill Myers, and how that all related to the dead guy in Johnny's cabin. I showered, brushed my teeth, and checked out of the motel.

The town of Battle Lake was beautiful and humming, the lake skirting the north edge of town sparkling in the sunlight, and it felt good to be heading back to the library where there was some order. I left my car in the motel parking lot near Dolly's and walked the three blocks to work. It was the Monday after the Fourth of July, so the town was packed with tourists up for the week. Families in brightly colored sundresses and T-shirts walked the streets, stopping at the Apothecary for sunscreen and mosquito repellent, window shopping at the local stores that wouldn't open for another hour. I strolled along with a little grin on my face.

I felt good enough to treat myself to iced green tea and a bagel at the Fortune Café. The coffee shop was packed. I waited my turn and was greeted by Sid's smiling face.

"You look like the cat who got the mouse."

"I hope to be the chick who gets the Native American. What's the word on the street?"

Sid shook her head. "It doesn't look so good for your love interests. First, Wenonga, and now a dead body at Johnny's cabin. You're not Irish, are you?"

"You know anything about that dead body at Johnny's cabin?"

"Just that it was scalped. Not so good for business. You want some iced tea?"

"Please, green sweetened. And a bagel with olive cream cheese, to go." I glanced around at the crowd filling her shop. "Your business seems to be doing fine."

Sid scooped a pile of ice into a disposable cup. "Most of these people just got to town. If word spreads that it's not safe, I don't know what's going to happen. The only good news is that the dead guy isn't local."

"That's not good news to a tourist, I suppose." I smiled and traded cash for food and drink. I threaded my way back through the crowd, wondering what sort of tourists Battle Lake would start drawing if this murder wasn't solved soon. It really wouldn't be good for business, and a lot of people I cared about were doing business in Battle Lake. That gave me one more reason to solve this murder. I sipped my tea and walked into the library with a spring in my step. The front room was just as clean as I had left it, and the air-conditioned oxygen felt refreshing against my face. I tossed my keys on the front counter, eyeballed the stack of books in the dropbox that needed shelving, and whistled as I headed to the back room to check my messages. It might have been the start of a perfect day if not for the man in my rear office, buck naked but for an Indian headdress and some war paint.

TWENTY-ONE

I'M NOT ASHAMED TO say I screamed, for the second time in under a week. At the sound of my shriek, the man jumped behind my desk and crouched down, his face redder than the paint streaked across his chest.

I darted forward to grab the stapler off my desk and lunged back, holding the implement like a white trash gun, staples out. "Who are you?"

He held his hands in front of him in the universal sign of "don't hurt me, this is a big misunderstanding." That's when Mrs. Berns came up from the basement. Her shirt was unbuttoned down the front, revealing a puckered bra, and her hair was disheveled. Around her waist, she had a gun belt strung low, capshooters stuck in each of the holsters.

She looked annoyed to see me. "It's Sunday. Even God rested on Sunday. Don't you have any social life?"

I looked from the naked guy crouched behind my desk to Mrs. Berns, and back again to the naked guy. "It's Monday, Mrs. Berns. What's going on?"

"Monday? Well, put a hitch in my giddy-up! We've been playing cowboys and Indians for two whole days, Bill! No wonder I was so hungry."

A hangdog Bill was gathering loose paper off my desk to cover his pork and beans, and something was dawning on me. "Bill? Not Bill Myers, by any chance?"

He stood, clutching an invoice across his privates, and sheepishly offered me a hand. "None other. Sorry for the scare."

I have a rule against shaking hands with naked men, one that I have to invoke far more often than you'd think. I put my fists on my hips instead. "Do you know the whole town is looking for you? They thought you were kidnapped from the parade."

Mrs. Berns pulled out a gun and let a pop into the air, cackling. "He was! I got him!"

A ridiculous thought dawned on me. If Mrs. Berns had taken Bill, did that mean she had also taken the Chief? "Mrs. Berns, you didn't take the big Indian too, did you?"

"They come in different sizes?"

"I meant Chief Wenonga."

"Hell no, girl. What would I do with a big fiberglass statue? Billy here is all the man I need."

"No shit?"

"Not even a little turd."

I let out a breath. There was one crime solved. Mrs. Berns had absconded with poor Bill Myers and had been having her way with him since Friday night. The two Native Americans disappearing in as many days were unrelated. "Good. Well, Billy better get some clothes on and tell Gary Wohnt that he's all right. And I'll thank you to keep the library out of your love life in the future."

"My tax dollars pay for this library, too, little missy, so as long as I have a library card, I will use it as I please."

I knew Mrs. Berns had keys to nearly every business in Battle Lake (thanks mostly to a bad habit of stealing the spares), so there was no point in arguing. "Can you two just take it elsewhere? I have to open up in forty-five minutes."

"Party pooper. You're just lucky it's snack time at the Sunset. I'll be back around lunchtime to help you with the tourist rush."

"Thank you, Mrs. Berns."

"Oh hey, get any new obituaries in the *Recall* the last coupla days? Folks at the Sunset get mad if I don't tell them who died and they have to find out from the newspaper."

"No new obits that I know of."

Mrs. Berns looked thoughtful as she buttoned up the front of her blouse. "You know how I'd like to go? One of those stuttering strokes. A little notice and then you're gone. That's what Lydia Thorfinnson had, that lucky old coot."

"If you ever do die, I'm sure you'll do it with style."

That seemed to satisfy her, and she headed toward the door. I kept busy shelving books and watering plants, and was careful not to make eye contact with Mr. Myers as he scurried out the door. Out of the corner of my eye, I noticed he looked a little saddle sore, but Mrs. Berns seemed none the worse for the wear. As soon as I had the library ready for business, I unlocked the door and planted myself at the front computer. I needed to send 1,500 words to Ron Sims by today, and he wanted it in three articles. The first piece would summarize the mundane parts of Wenonga Days and the second one would focus on the missing statue, but what would the third article be about? I figured it would be best to start writing and see what came. First, the Wenonga Days straight stuff.

"Annual Wenonga Days Festival Well-Attended"

This year, Wenonga Days started with a bang. Although the Chief missed his own celebration, he was there in spirit throughout the weekend. Crazy Days on Friday brought in a crowd of people shopping for bargains as every business on Lake Street offered discounts from 25–75 percent off original prices.

Friday evening, an estimated 400 people attended the street dance to hear "Not with My Horse," a band out of Minneapolis, serenade the crowd with their unique country punk fusion. The Rusty Nail sponsored the street dance.

For those who were up early Saturday, the Battle Lake Jaycees offered a Kiddie Karnival, Turtle Races, and a parade during the day. Ashley Grosbain's turtle was the clear winner at the races. The parade featured marching bands from all over Minnesota, Dalton's Antique Thresher review, and as a special surprise, Mayor Kennie Rogers and her group of radical cheerleaders, calling themselves "The Beaver Pelts," shared their moves with the crowd.

Also present at the parade was Brando Erikkson, owner of the fiberglass company that created Chief Wenonga. At the parade, Mr. Erikkson offered to donate a slightly irregular fiberglass woodchuck to replace the Wenonga statue.

The woodchuck will be delivered to Halvorson Park early this week.

The Saturday night fireworks, made possible due to the annual fundraiser put on by the Battle Lake Chamber of Commerce, were a big hit with families who viewed them from Glendalough Park. The display cost nearly $20,000 and lasted twenty-five minutes. There were no reported injuries.

The winner of Sunday's bike race in the female category was Linda Clarkson; the winner in the male category was Erik Schultz. Nikki Welde was the winner of the 5K run in the female category; Jerome Teske was the winner in the male category.

There was a grand turnout for the Pet and Owner Look-Alike Contest, but only one pair could win. This year, that lucky pair was Bill Green of Urbank and Kasey, his Golden Retriever.

The All-Town Garage sale offered a backdrop to Sunday's races. From start to finish, it's going to be hard to top this year's Wenonga Days.

I hit "save" and sat back in my captain's chair. Writing the first article wasn't too hard. Now, it was time to write the article about the missing Chief. I would build off my earlier draft.

"It's My Party, and I'll Fly if I Want To"

In a strange turn of events, Chief Wenonga disappeared from Battle Lake on Friday, July 3, just as the plans for his twenty-fifth birthday party were finalized. Police on the scene Friday morning found only four posts and what appeared to be blood at the Halvorson Park location where the Chief had stood proudly for twenty-five years.

Battle Lake was named by Chief Wenonga for a mêlée between the Ojibwe and Sioux that took place more than 200 years ago. The Sioux were encroaching on Ojibwe territory, and the Ojibwe leader, Ukkewaus, gathered nearly fifty warriors to fight for their land.

Although Ukkewaus and his warriors believed they were staging a surprise attack, the Sioux were prepared, and many Ojibwe died. Chief Wenonga led the remaining warriors back to Leech Lake, where he lived to an old age and was greatly respected by his tribe. The Battle Lake Civic and Commerce Club ordered the Wenonga statue in 1979 and initially placed it at the Y in Battle Lake. In 1986, the Chief was moved to Halvorson Park, where he stood until his disappearance last Friday.

In what appears to be a connected case, the dead body of an unidentified male was found in a cabin north of Battle Lake on Saturday evening. A local teenager found the body. Battle Lake Police are calling this case a homicide and are currently following up on several leads.

Battle Lake has recently been the site of several strange occurrences, including the May murder of Battle Lake alumnus Jeff Wilson. That mystery was solved soon after, and it is the hope of the people of Battle Lake that this latest case will be resolved soon also, so the town can return to normal.

I didn't know if "return" was an accurate word to use in the final paragraph, but I was too busy dealing with the hot slice of pain that came with typing Jeff's name to change it. I had been head to toe in love with him, and he was gone forever. Me and men. Maybe I could hire myself out to heartbroken women who had been dumped by or couldn't get rid of cheaters, abusers, emotional withholders, and the foreplay-challenged. After their mistreating man had a few dates with me, the problem would be solved. I'd call it the Jinx Man-away Service, and Kennie Rogers could be my business manager. Come to think of it, maybe Mrs. Berns could get involved, too.

I flicked my cheek to turn off the inner crazy-talk and refocused on my computer. I had two articles down and one more to write, and I had no blessed idea what it was going to be about. I sipped at my aromatic jasmine tea, still warm, and felt inspiration glide down my throat.

"Battle Lake Has Beauty and Backbone"

The village of Battle Lake officially came into existence Halloween, 1881, when it was platted for Torger O. and Bertie O. Holdt. By 1885, there were 182 residents of the village, but newspaper references at the time allude to unusual amounts of bad luck being visited on the inhabitants—mysterious plagues, crop rot, and intense weather were only the beginning.

The first white settlers found Native American mounds scattered in the region, forty-two near the lake's inlet alone. Local legend had it that whoever took over the land that had once belonged to the Indians would be cursed. In the last few months, it is hard to ignore the spectre of a curse as the town has contended with three murders in as many months—Jeff Wilson found dead in the library in May, a carnival gone horribly awry in June, and now the missing Chief Wenonga statue and homicide in July.

Although it is easy to write Battle Lake off as cursed, it would be a mistake. The town offers relaxation and warm smiles to travelers in the summer and is a full-service town with a dentist, chiropractor, and clinic open year-round, as well as the Village Apothecary available to meet the sundry and pharmaceutical needs of locals and tourists alike. The town also has an excellent newspaper to keep readers in touch with the local news.

Battle Lake has unique stores in which to window shop or find that special present, from the Bramble and the Rose to O'kay Gifts. Granny's Pantry sells ice cream cones bigger than your head and old-fashioned candy by the basket, and the Fortune Café has the best homemade ginger scones in the county.

If you're one of the few not lucky enough to catch sunnies and trophy walleyes for supper, delicious food is easy to find in Battle Lake, from the eggs Benedict at the Shoreline to the tator tot hotdish at the Turtle Stew to the butterknife steaks and fresh-baked bread at Stub's.

If you're only in town for a while, there are more than thirty safe, clean, and fun places to stay, from Xanadu Island Resort to the Battle Lake Motel to the Nifty Nook Resort. If you're in town for longer, the streets are safe, the schools are good, and the community is united. Battle Lake may have gotten a rough start and had its share of misfortunes, but the town remains strong in the face of it all. Battle Lake is, after all, easy to get to and hard to leave.

I winced at my last sentence—it is hard to leave any place when you're dead—but I felt good about the article. A lot of good people were working and running businesses in Battle Lake, and they shouldn't be punished just because a few crazies had found their way here. I meant every word I had typed. I saved all three articles and emailed them as attachments, just as the phone rang.

"James, where are my articles?"

"Hi, Ron. It's not noon yet. That was my deadline."

"Deadlines are for the weak and undisciplined. Where are my articles?"

"They are plummeting through cyberspace and into your computer as we speak. Maybe I should get a raise?"

"Maybe you should get me a new recipe for next week's paper. People can't get enough of that garbage you find. I don't know how you do it."

"It's a gift. Say, whaddya know about the dead body found out at Johnny's cabin?"

A reluctant grunt traveled through the wire. "Can you keep a secret?"

Technically, I wouldn't be lying if I said yes because I could *theoretically* keep a secret, even if I might not keep *this* secret. "You know it."

"I don't know it, and if you spill this before Wohnt makes it public, you're out one reporting job. The corpse didn't have any ID on it, but a wallet washed up in Silver Lake, and the photo and vital stats on the driver's license found in it seems to match the corpse. His name was Liam Anderson, he was from Wausau, Wisconsin, and that's all I know."

Wausau? Why did that sound familiar? I had never been, and I didn't think I knew anyone from there. Dolly and Brando were from Stevens Point. It might be worth my time to find out how close that city was to Wausau. I still needed to get back out to Johnny's cabin too, but that would have to wait until I closed the library at 6:00. "Thanks for the tip. I'll keep it close to my chest."

Ron grunted. "Just get me a recipe before the end of the week. Friday is the end of the week."

The phone went *click*, and I was alone in the library. I went to Rand McNally online and learned that Wausau was 361 miles east of Battle Lake, but Stevens Point was only 34 miles from Wausau. That was a little too close for comfort. I felt woozy wondering if I could really trust Johnny at his word, that he had been in Stevens Point only to dig up dirt on Dolly. The more I thought about it, the more I realized he could have been feeding me a whole zoo full of lyin'. The library door opened with a pleasant *dong*, and I looked up anxiously. It was a woman and three children, all under the age of ten. I smiled at them and exited the map program.

While they browsed the children's section, I went back to reshelving books. A steady crowd continued until lunchtime, and I was so busy answering questions that time flew. When Mrs. Berns came in at 1:00, I was starving. I decided to ignore the fact that I had only hours earlier seen her at the afterglow stage of a weekend sexcapade. "Hi, Mrs. Berns. Hope you came ready to work. We're busy today."

Mrs. Berns looked sprightly and innocent, her eyes wide and blue and her apricot hair still in curlers. She was wearing a Shania

Twain concert T-shirt, cut-off jean shorts, and orthopedic shoes. "I've been working it since I was born, girl."

"OK. Do you mind if I run and get some lunch?"

"Nope. But I thought you might want to run to Fergus Falls instead."

I eyed her suspiciously. She began straightening out the pencils on the front desk. "Why?"

"They arrested your boy toy, Johnny Leeson. I thought maybe you could squeeze in a conjugal visit before they send him on to Folsom."

I felt myself shrink, sucked into a hole that was starting in my own stomach. "What?"

She scowled at me. "Don't act so surprised. As soon as you so much as look sideways at a guy, his life is in the shitter. You got an evil eye, girl. You should maybe consider keeping those legs together and that mind on something clean, like the Bible or charity work. You're bad luck ten ways from Sunday."

I stood like a leather-skinned zombie until the hot tears in my eyes cracked through. "You're right."

Mrs. Berns stopped straightening the front counter and looked at me, fire in her face. "What? You're going to give up like that? I ain't *right*. I'm just a bitchy old woman. We all make our own luck, so don't just roll over like a dog in heat. Go fix this. Go. I'll watch the library."

"I don't know, Mrs. Berns. Maybe it'd be better if I—"

"Shut your piehole with the 'I don't know.' Go. You found Jeff's murderer, you got rid of that terrible Jason Blunt, and now you're going to spring Johnny Leeson. Let me know if you need help, by the way. I've always wanted to break into a prison."

"But what if he's guilty?" There. I had said it out loud, and it felt good.

She turned on me, fire in her eyes. "I'll tell you this only one time, Mira James. I know you've had a tough life, but you're not the only one, so get over it. If you start chasing shadows and mistrusting everyone, you're going to miss the best life has to offer. Now, do you honestly think Johnny Leeson murdered someone?"

I blinked once, twice, my mouth open. After scouring my heart and head I made room for the possibility that Johnny had been up front with me, except for the lapse when he drove to Stevens Point to investigate Dolly. But could I really consider trusting him? I didn't feel good about giving another man an opportunity to hurt me. There's bad luck, and then there's just stupidity. I was too young to be responsible for my dad, and I was willing to chalk Jeff up to fickle fate, but the other men in my life hadn't exactly been model partners. There was Bad Brad, of course. The cheater. Before him was Kyle, from my hometown, who I had run into in the Cities and started dating during my sophomore year of college. I had thought I was in love with him, but he was so afraid of commitment that he wouldn't even change the subject lines on emails before replying—figured it would lead me on by showing undue attention. Sprinkled among that love life detritus were various bad dates, including but not limited to a post-operative transsexual and a guy who peed uphill on the Astroturf of the fifteenth hole of the golf course on our first date. In his defense, it was a long course. For mini golf.

No, if I took Johnny's side, and he turned out to be a liar, I wouldn't be able to trust myself again. Unfortunately, my other option was to let him twist in the wind and hope that Wohnt caught the real murderer soon. *Shit*. I kicked at the carpeting, feeling Mrs. Berns' eyes on me. Why couldn't I just be one of those chicks whose biggest worry is what shoes go with her cute sundress, and the fifty-two best ways to flirt? Instead, I had to decide whether or not to help the hot guy who may or may not be lying to me about the dead body in his dad's cabin. *Shit*.

I made up my mind. "No, I don't think he killed anyone. But—"

"Shush. Go. Sissy crybaby girl."

I didn't know if she was trying to make me feel better or worse, but she was right that I couldn't stay here and worry about Johnny in jail all day. I was going out to his cabin and see what I could find to fix all this.

TWENTY-TWO

I WAS INFINITELY LESS optimistic and Snow Whitey-birds-land-ing-on-my-shoulders on my way back to my car in the Battle Lake Motel parking lot than I had been leaving it. I took the time to notice that Dolly's car was gone and wondered where a woman who was in town only to protest Chief Wenonga Days went once the statue and those days were gone. I suppose that depended on whether or not she had accomplished her mission. Should I try tracking her down and tailing her? Do people tail each other anymore, and did they ever on the plains of Minnesota? I filed that away as a "consider later" action.

I made my way to Silver Lake and was not surprised to see the yellow and black police tape streamed across Johnny's drive-way. Fortunately, there were no police in sight, so I parked my car a hundred or so feet from the entrance and hoofed it back. My working theory was that Dolly, Brando, and the freshly deceased Liam Anderson had removed Chief Wenonga for some unknown reason. Their deal went sour, and when Liam threatened to turn them in, Dolly and Brando killed him, putting a chunk of his scalp on the base of the statue as some sort of message. I knew Johnny had been to his place Saturday afternoon to set up the balloons, so they must have stashed the corpse out here sometime between then and when I found it Sunday morning. Why they chose Johnny's cabin was still a mystery.

I walked to the end of the driveway and ducked under the crime scene tape. The pile of paint-soaked leaves looked like it had been meticulously dug through, and when I poked around with my toe, I didn't see any balloon fragments remaining. The grass between the paint trap and the cabin was trampled flat, and I didn't spend any time looking at the ground. I had come to see the cabin, to see if I had missed anything on my terror-soaked visit yesterday.

Goosebumps rose on my arms, the chilling effect unsettling in the oppressive heat. What if the body was still in there, the white foot starting to decompose in the humid air? I pinched my cheek. That was ridiculous. There was no body in there. The police had removed all evidence, and this was probably just a fool's errand so I should get it over and done with. I marched to the cabin and walked around the perimeter. Glancing in the first window, I saw that the bed had been stripped clean and the mattress removed. I followed the shape of the cabin until I was at the front entrance.

The door had been removed and was not in sight. Police tape crisscrossed the gaping hole, and I felt an itch at the back of my brain. It had to do with the door, but it wasn't coming clearly. I stepped forward, peeking around the tape, and imagined I could still smell a coppery tinge of blood floating out of the cabin. I considered breaking through the tape, and that's when I scratched the itch: whoever had put the body in Johnny's cabin had broken in, nearly taking the door off its hinges in the process. If Johnny had been involved, he would not have had to break in. Whoever had left the body had either been setting him up, or had just been looking for a quiet spot to leave the man. Now I could believe it.

I turned to breathe in the fresh air of the forest.

TWENTY-THREE

I DROVE BACK INTO town to the Fortune Café. Some iced coffee would do nicely to clear my head. Or at least it would have, if I hadn't run into Brando outside. His sleek black hair was in a ponytail, and his skin glowed bronze in the July sun. He wore a short-sleeved, button-down shirt in plaid, khaki shorts that skimmed his knees, and brown fisherman sandals.

"Hey, little bird! You look hot."

I scowled. Did he mean hot as in good or hot as in sweaty? "I am hot."

"Yeah, this weather is something else. Did you hear? The chipmunk statue is being delayed. It won't be here until next week. Bad news."

"Chipmunk? I thought it was a woodchuck."

"Chipmunk, woodchuck," he said, in a "tomato, tomahto" voice, as he sidled up next to me. "That means I won't be here to see it installed. Wanna have a going-away party for me?"

I started to pull away from him, and then forced myself to stand still. If I was going to help Johnny, and I had decided I had no choice but to help Johnny as a *friend*, I needed to find out what was up with Brando and Dolly. "What did you have in mind?" I tried looking down submissively at his feet and then back into his eyes because I read somewhere that gesture is appealing to the primal hunter in every man, but I'm pretty sure I just looked like I had something in my eye.

"I'm staying at a cabin outside of town, but it's really messy, and I have to be out of there by today, anyways. How about I come over to your place tonight?"

He tried to play with a tendril of my hair, but hesitated when he realized it was sweat soaked. I distracted him with my brightest smile. "That would be great! I'll make us supper. What do you like to eat?"

Brando winked. "Eating is one of my favorite parts of slumber parties."

Boy, was this guy transparent or what? "Great, I'll grill some tofu and vegetables. You bring a couple bottles of wine."

He raised his eyebrow. "I like a girl who's not afraid to drink. Where do you live?"

I gave him directions and instead of entering the café, I bopped down to Larry's to pick up some tofu. I decided to go home and marinate it and pick up the house, but first I made a run past the motel. Still no Dolly car.

I cruised home into the wagging tails and warm eyes of my animals. Actually, Tiger Pop only sniffed in my direction, but I could see the restrained welcome in his eyes. He was happy I was here. Luna, like most dogs, was a whore for love and jumped up on me like I was the last Krispy Kreme outside a Weight Watchers grand opening.

"You guys miss me? Hunh? You guys miss me?" I scratched them both behind their ears and didn't let up on Tiger Pop until he purred, against his will. I scooped their food, poured them ice water, filled the bird feeders, and hosed out and refreshed the birdbath. I considered setting the sprinkler in the garden, but it was still 103 degrees, according to my thermometer, and the water would evaporate before it'd soak in. I made a mental note to put the sprinkler out after dark.

Tasks done, I went inside and set my Stun Gun to charge. Then, I sliced and marinated the tofu in Bragg's and garlic chili paste and slipped it in the fridge. The chilled air from the refrigerator felt heavenly, though it smelled like old cilantro and dill pickles. I dusted, vacuumed, scooped out the litter box, and watered my plants before hopping in a cold shower. In less than two hours, the house and I were clean, but I still hadn't decided what to wear. I wanted to be attractive to loosen his tongue, but I also didn't want to provide easy access to any erogenous zones. I opted for a push-up bra under a button-front, short-sleeved white peasant shirt, open to the third button.

For my bottom half, I debated wearing underwear but couldn't bring myself to do it no matter how badly I wanted the extra layer. It was too hot, and underwear under jeans or pants had always felt like wearing diapers to me. I compromised and slipped on cut-off, button-fly Levis. I slid a delicate silver chain around my left ankle, thin silver hoops in each ear, and dusted sandalwood perfume on my wrists and behind my knees. I twisted my hair into a loose bun at the base of my neck, artfully pulling tendrils down around my face. A little eyeliner, mascara, and lip gloss, and I was as cute as I was going to get.

Just in time, too. I heard Luna bark as the red Hummer pulled up. I couldn't believe I was letting a man who drove a Humvee into my home. The things a gal has to do for her friends.

Brando parked the red tank under the towering lilacs in the middle circle of the driveway and emerged, standing on his running board like the captain of the Titanic. He wore the same button-down shirt and khaki shorts he had been in earlier, but his hair was loose around his shoulders and so black it looked blue in the sun. "Beautiful place you have here."

"Thank you."

After he was sure I had a chance to admire him, top to bottom, astride his gas-guzzling, metal Viagra, he reached in for two bottles of wine and hopped down. "Hope you like Pinot Grigio."

I liked it better than I liked him. "Is it cold?"

"Like ice." He drew out the sibilance of the last word, like a snake.

"Come on in. I'll get some glasses."

I led the way into the house but was pulled up short by his low wolf whistle. "That is a *beautiful* view."

Something told me he wasn't talking about the lake on the other side of my garden, so I ignored the comment. I held the door for him so he had to enter the house in front of me. "Want to help me get the grill going?"

"Oooh, no can do. I'm a restaurant kind of man. Don't know much about grilling. I can open wine, though." He offered me a playful smile.

The effort it took not to roll my eyes almost made me lose my balance, but I managed. I tossed him a wine opener before I went out to light the charcoal. "Glasses are in the cupboard, above the sink." I felt his eyes burn holes into my ass as I walked outside.

"Stop looking at me like that," I hissed at Tiger Pop, as he criticized me from his sunspot on the back deck. "It's not what you think." He closed his eyes in half-lidded judgment. Luna just looked at me eagerly, if a little sadly, as if to say, "Us easy chicks need to stick together, right?" I sighed and turned on the gas grills, tossing a wooden match at it from a safe distance. I had lost my eyebrows lighting a gas stove as a child and had not gotten within three feet of fuel with flame since. Usually, by the twelfth or thirteenth air-lobbed match, I'd have the grill going, and tonight was no exception.

"Beautiful night," Brando said as he opened the screen door with his hip, a glass of wine in each hand. "And beautiful company."

I reached for the wine, downed half the glass, and smiled up at him. "How long do you plan to stay in Battle Lake?"

"Don't you remember? Tonight is my going-away party."

I pulled away from his seeking hand. "So you're leaving tomorrow?"

"I have a little business to take care of," he said vaguely. "When it's done, I'll be gone. Shouldn't take more'n a day or two."

"What kind of business? You made friends in town?"

He smirked. "I have friends everywhere. That grill ready? I'm a hungry man."

I wondered at the change of subject as I strolled past him into the house. I threw back the rest of my wine, refilled my glass, and grabbed the marinated tofu and the vegetables I had skewered and piled them on a tray. Except for the mushrooms and red peppers, the vegetables were fresh from my garden—baby potatoes, new onions, miniature zucchini, and cherry tomatoes I had bought as nearly full-grown plants from Johnny at the greenhouse. I also grabbed the grilling tray that was meant for fish but that I used to keep the tofu from sticking to my grill when I turned it. I balanced the food and my wine glass on the tray on my right hand and opened the door with my left. "Coming through!"

"That looks delicious. You're kind of a granola gal, aren't you, what with all your fresh veggies and your long hair? I love au naturel girls."

I put down the tray, slammed my second glass of wine as he strolled closer, and held my empty glass like a wall between the two of us. "Can you fill this? You might need to open a new bottle."

He looked momentarily surprised, and then smiled brightly. "No problem."

While he was in the house, I sprayed down the grill and set out the veggies and tofu. He returned shortly with a refreshed glass of wine for me. "Thank you."

"You're welcome. I'm really glad you invited me out here today, Myra."

"It's Mira, like, 'you better stand clear-a.'"

"Mira. Of course. Battle Lake is a quirky little town, you know, and all you people have made me feel so welcome. I might just have to return some day real soon." He set down his wine glass and stood behind me. I forced myself to stand still, like a deer who doesn't want to run from the hunter too soon and expose herself, and I didn't even flinch when he started to massage my shoulders.

In fact, it soon began to feel tolerable, even good, cresting on the warm buzz of a wine high. "You like that, don't you, Mira? You're so tense, and you carry it all in your shoulders. I can feel it melting away now. Can't you?"

I closed my eyes and let my head roll slightly. I really could feel the tension leaving and the warm buzz of wine filling in the cracks. What luck, that the guy with the Hummer has magic hands. The tofu popped, and so did my eyes. I turned the vegetables and tofu slabs, but with minimal movement on my part so as not to interrupt the massage. "I have been stressed lately," I offered reluctantly, reaching to take a deep swallow from my third glass of wine. My head started to swim pleasantly.

"I'm sure," he growled soothingly into my ear. "Running the library, writing for the newspaper, keeping the town safe. It's a full-time job. You're a real beauty, you know, Mira." His hands trailed my spine to its base and went back up again, his fingers strong and seeking.

My eyes were half-lidded, which was all I needed to see that the food was done. I pulled it off the grill, disappointed but relieved that my massage was going to end. I needed to keep my head on straight if I wanted to come out of this interview on top, or at least with my clothes intact. "Do you want to eat inside or outside?"

I turned to him, holding the tray of food, and was surprised by the hooded intensity in his eyes. He took the tray out of my hands and set it down on the picnic table by the grill. Before I could object, he pulled my face to his and brushed his mouth against me. His lips were strong, and when I instinctively leaned my body into his, they softened and fit to me perfectly. I could feel the taut length of him and a tremor passed through me. I tried to muster

176

up indignation, outrage, or even disgust at how easy I was, but this guy was *good*. He seemed to have eight hands, in the best possible way. I wondered if he was like olives. You had to work really hard to like them, but once you did, you couldn't get enough.

For a split second, common sense commandeered the steering wheel and I tried to pull away, but one hand at the small of my back and the other tangled in my hair tugged me back into him, hard. Our kissing was the real deal—no teeth scraping, no awkward tongue wrestling, no unintentional noises. I could taste the sweet flavor of wine on his lips and tongue. Research, I would call this. He would certainly be much more relaxed with me after we fooled around, and maybe I could get him to spill some secrets then. I hoped Johnny would appreciate what I was doing to set him free. *Johnny.* I stepped back, quickly, and looked into Brando's surprisingly unfamiliar face. What the hell had I been doing? "Um, maybe we should eat."

He cocked his head, like a bird, and studied me clinically. I suddenly felt very uneasy. "Sure. Let's eat." He ran his fingers through his hair, never taking his cold eyes off me.

I picked up the food but was sure to my bones that I did not want to turn my back on this man. I didn't know what had triggered the sudden shift from passion to anger, but I could feel fury radiating from him like heat waves. I saw Luna stand up behind him, the hackles raised on her neck. "You first."

It might have been a stand-off, if not for the bile-green Gremlin that grunted down my driveway. Both Brando and I watched it pull up and park behind the Humvee.

"Holy shit! What the fuck is that? Are we at war?" Brad snort-laughed as he stepped out of his rusty car and walked admiringly around the Humvee. No longer in a lab coat, he wore a tank top that highlighted his farmer's tan and a pair of cut-offs. "These are some cherry wheels."

I watched Brando out of the corner of my eye. Both his anger and his pants deflated slowly but steadily, as if by sheer force of will. By the time Brad reached us, Brando was his suave, good-looking self again. He offered his hand to Brad. "Those are my wheels, and thank you. Name's Brando."

"No shit? That's a great name. I'm Brad."

I could see the wheels turning in Brad's head, or, more accurately, "wheel," and I foresaw a name change in the near future for the leader of "Not with My Horse." I was too grateful to see Brad to make fun of him, though. "Hey, Brad. You're just in time. We were about to eat. You hungry?"

"You know I can always eat. As long as you guys don't mind. We can celebrate my good news!"

"What's your good news?"

"It looks like I found a job. When I was down at Bonnie & Clyde's, I heard they're hiring construction workers in Fergus Falls, or I could bartend at Stub's, and some guy even told me there is a crazy professor in town paying good money for workers to tear down statues."

Brando and I looked at each other. His face was unreadable, and I hoped mine was too. More likely, however, my right ear looked like a "D," my right eye looked like an "O," the furrowed lines between my brows looked like two "Ls," and my left eyebrow looked like a "Y."

Brando brushed his hand across his mouth and leaned in to kiss my forehead. I winced, whether from the leftover heat between us or fear, I wasn't sure. "Thanks for inviting me out, Mira, but I better be getting back to town. I have some packing that I need to finish."

"Sure, Brando. Maybe some other time."

He gave Brad a curt nod, fired up the tank, and was out the driveway in a dramatic rumble.

"What the fuck is he driving, anyhow? A 1057 All-Desert 10-ton Dune Runner?"

"It's a Humvee, Brad." Now that Brando was gone, I wanted Brad gone, too. I had been through a lot the last couple days, and to top it all off, I could feel a thwarted-sex headache forming behind my eyes. "I appreciate you coming when you did, by the way. I'm really tired, though. Can I pack some food up for you to take with?"

Brad looked at me, seriously looked at me, for the first time since he had been in town. "You do look beat. Why don't you go lay down? I'll bring the food in and take what I need."

His sudden kindness brought my guilt for making out with Brando to the surface. I took a stab at easing it by clearing up a bad mark from my past. "You know how I left Minneapolis without saying goodbye?"

Brad nodded, his mouth full of tofu.

"It was because I caught you cheating on me. With Ted's dog-sitter."

He swallowed and looked at me sheepishly. "I kinda figured. I'm sorry."

"And I took the nuts off your bike, which is why you crashed it."

Brad started laughing. "No shit? That hurt."

I smiled back at him, relieved by his reaction. "Yeah, well, it was pretty childish, and I'm sorry I did it."

"I deserved it," he said, grabbing for another piece of tofu.

"Thanks, Brad." I was in the house and asleep in my bed before he left.

TWENTY-FOUR

WHEN MY EYES OPENED, the birds were singing but the sky was dark. I sat up and my bed swayed under me. The digital clock on my nightstand was blinking 12:00 in an acid red, meaning the power had gone out at some point, and a rip of thunder rolled across the lake and into the house. My heart caromed off its track and hammered around loose in my chest. Was it Monday night or Tuesday morning? How long had I been asleep? Was I alone in my house?

The smell of ozone, followed by a flash of lightning, was unsettling. I forced myself out of the bed and into my kitchen. The battery-powered clock hanging on a nail over the fridge read 7:36, but I still didn't know if it was AM or PM. What time had I gone to bed? I scratched at my head and jumped as Tiger Pop brushed against my leg.

"Hey, sweetie. How long have I been asleep?" No answer. I went to my front door, which had been shut and locked. Brad, looking out for me, about a year too late. I opened the inner door and leaned my face against the cool screen. It must be morning, or the screen would still be warm. I watched the first drop of rain hit my garden, scaring up black dust. Then the second drop came, and the third, and as I belatedly realized I had left my car windows open, the sky opened up and emptied her tubs. I ran to my car, rolled up all four windows, and was drenched right down to the inner crotch seam of my cut-offs by the time I splashed back inside. As the rain pounded down, a wicked cold breeze slipped like an icy tongue through the wall of heavy air, and I knew we were in for a mother of a storm.

"Whaddya think, Tiger Pop? Should I wait it out, or make a run for town now before it gets even worse?"

"Whoof," Luna said. To town it was. I considered my run to the car a shower, so I only needed to change clothes and brush my teeth. I got Luna and Tiger Pop fresh food and water and, umbrella in hand, put their vittles in the sheltered area under the house. I also relocated a disgruntled Tiger Pop to that area. When the rain let up, I knew they'd both want to be outside.

My house was still tidy, so there was nothing to do but go into the storm and drive. The sky was black, except for the razors of lightning that cut through it, and the thunder was the only sound loud enough to trump the shovelfuls of rain hammering down. Battle Lake was getting itself cleaned behind the ears, sure enough, and I knew the farmers were going to be elated, as long as no hail came with the package. Their crazy high corn needed to be watered.

The drive to town was slow. At thirty miles per hour, I could just barely make out the hood of my car, and my windshield wipers were doing more stirring than removing of rain. Sid and Nancy, bless their hearts, had the Fortune Café open when I arrived at 8:30, but there wasn't much business in town. The only other customers in the café were some out-of-towners and their miserable-looking kids ("But honey, we can play Monopoly in here until the rain lets up!"), Les Pastner, and a waitress from the Turtle Stew ordering some real coffee before her shift started.

I stepped in line behind the waitress but was distracted by the sound of radio snaps and burps. Les was at the two-top table to my immediate left, fiddling with a small radio poorly hidden in his jacket. To my infinite surprise, he looked to be drinking a marble mocha macchiato, extra whipped cream, hold the cinnamon. Apparently, even militia men are not immune to the finer pleasures life has to offer.

"What're you listening to, Les?"

"Police scanner."

"Any news?"

"Can't hear. The storm is messing up my frequency."

"Mind if I join you after I get my breakfast?"

Les' hair was slicked off to one side with a part you could land a jet on, and his squinty eyes were so deep-set, I couldn't tell what color they were, though the green-gray of his eye bags reflected off their surface. Right now, he looked at me as if I had asked him if I could paint his toenails pink. "Why?"

"You and me need to talk."

He looked around furtively. The waitress had taken her coffee and left, and Sid and Nancy had politely disappeared into the kitchen. Meanwhile, the family had settled into the back room to see if the Parker Brothers could keep them sane. "You said you weren't gonna tell no one you saw me outside the motel." His voice sounded accusing.

"And I meant it. I just want to know if you found out anything else about Dolly and Brando. Did they come to town together?"

Les tried to look tough, like an impenetrable gangsta, but it wasn't an easy look to pull off with whipped cream on your upper lip and a macchiato in hand. "I'm not working for you."

That set me back on my heels. Les had tipped his hand a little too far. "But you're working for someone." It was a statement, not a question. "Who?"

He took another sip of his gourmet coffee and busied himself fiddling with his radio.

"OK, don't tell me who it is. What'd they hire you to do?"

A clear stream of words came out of the radio, though it sounded distant. Les pulled up the antennae and readjusted them like they were metal chopsticks and he was trying to pick up a tiny ball of rice.

"Was it a male or female who hired you, or both?"

"…Big Ole statue missing from Alexandria…"

Les' eyes got big, and he tuned in the information stream cackling from the radio.

"It's just gone. What does someone want with a big Norwegian statue?"

There was a crackle, and then a response from another officer, or the dispatcher. "Ransom? Or maybe Chief Wenonga was getting lonely." Followed by a chuckle. "No scalp on this one?"

"No blood. I repeat, no blood. The statue has just disappeared."

I had been leaning into the radio and so jumped when Les slammed it against the tabletop, spilling his coffee. "God bless it!

This is not how it was supposed to go!" He ignored the mess he had made and stormed out of the Fortune Café, radio in hand.

Sid reappeared from the kitchen. "What was that all about?"

I shook my head in amazement. "Les' police scanner. Someone took Big Ole out of Alexandria."

"No way!" She wiped her hands on the towel she was carrying, and I was shocked to notice she was wearing a skirt. "Well, it looks like our bad luck is spreading around a little. But why is someone stealing schlocky statues?"

I bristled at the "schlocky," but made a joke of it. "Maybe they want to build the world's biggest mini golf course?" Inside, though, my thoughts were spinning. I had assumed that Chief Wenonga had been stolen to strike a blow for PEAS, and the missing Bill Myers dressed as a Native American had lent credence to that theory. Now, Bill had been found, and a non-Indian statue had been stolen. This was clearly about the statues, and not the politics, which pointed the finger squarely at Brando. But how was Dolly involved?

"I don't think it's for mini golf. Where do you hide twenty-plus-foot statues?"

Good question. "I dunno, Sid. Can I get a sun-dried tomato bagel with provolone cheese, to go? And maybe a Diet Coke. I have a feeling it's going to be a long day."

"Sure thing, shug." Sid wrapped my food in waxed paper and filled a to-go cup with pop, and I went back into the rain. It had let up from "firehose in the sky" to "water pressure in the average double-wide," so I gambled I wouldn't need my umbrella to dash the fifteen feet from the front door of the Fortune to my car. I lost that bet. I was soaked, for the second time that day. The temperature was 74 degrees, according to the bank's LCD screen, so at least it wasn't a miserable soaked.

I drove to the library and shook off inside. I fired up the front desk computer and began searching, starting with "Big Ole Alexandria Minnesota." The first link pulled up an attractive (if you like the Nordic type) picture of big Ole, horned-helmet on his head, blonde, shoulder-length locks cascading into his beard and moustache. He carried a wussy-looking spear in one hand and a shield in the other, with his sword strapped at his waist. He wore a skirt that would make Paris Hilton proud. It was bright yellow and skimmed the upper thighs of his unusually long legs. It also highlighted nicely the fact that one leg was raised and stepping forward, as if to say, "I have conquered this land, and I did it in a skirt." It was suggestively sexy, in a homoerotic sort of way. Me, I preferred tall, dark, and handsome. There was something nagging me about that statue, though. Something familiar.

I read the caption and was brought up to date on Alexandria history. The town called itself "The Birthplace of America," due to the Kensington runestone found nearby in 1898 under the roots of an aspen tree by Olaf Ohman, an illiterate local farmer. The markings on the 202-pound stone were believed to be a runic inscription describing a Viking expedition in 1362, a date well-preceding Columbus' "discovery" of America. Controversy followed the discovery, with Ohman's veracity being called into question.

In 1948, the Smithsonian displayed the runestone, where it stayed for about twenty years until the museum decided it was a fake, returning it to Minnesota. Unfortunately, the curators had scrubbed off with a wire brush all the microevidence that could have dated it. It was apparently quite a scandal, with differing conspiracy theories as to why the museum had scrubbed the stone.

Before the Smithsonian biffed and at the high point of the positive runestone publicity, Alexandria commissioned a twenty-eight-foot fiberglass statue of Ole Oppe, better known as the Viking, Big Ole. Big Ole began his existence at the World's Fair in 1964 before moving to Alexandria. I searched three more sites using "Big Ole" as the search term, and finally found what I was looking for under "Ole Oppe": the statue had been built by one Fibertastic Enterprises out of Stevens Point, Wisconsin.

Hello, Brando Erikkson. Why, pray tell, are you stealing your own statues? And why scalp Liam Anderson?

I flipped back to my computer and Googled "Fibertastic Enterprises." I had visited the site earlier, but had not dug deeply. This time, I was going to find something, even if I had to read all 1,314 hits. The first hit was the same home page for the Stevens Point company that I had come across in my original search. The next hundred or so were links to the websites of communities that had purchased statues from Fibertastic and were crediting the company. Among these were links to Chief Wenonga in Battle Lake and Big Ole in Alexandria. It was at link number 132 that I hit pay dirt in the form of a brief article in the online English version of the *Mumbai Mirror* out of Bombay. The article was titled "Gandhi Falls on Jain Passersby, Injuring Many":

A group of six Jain devotees, on a pilgrimage to Shatrunjaya Hills, were injured as the twenty-five-foot statue of Mahatma Gandhi they walked under fell on them. The statue had been commissioned in the late 1970s by a wealthy Brit

187

named Bobcat Perham and intended as a reminder of Gandhi's sacrifices. Fibertastic Enterprises, a Wisconsin, United States, company, built, shipped, and installed the statue. The statue's fall appeared to be an act of God.

The article included a picture of the Gandhi statue, presumably taken before it had toppled over. In the photograph, the statue looked unusually robust, given Gandhi's historically emaciated appearance, and strangely familiar. I contemplated that as I ran the name of the town through my memory. Shatrunjaya Hills. When Johnny had called from Wisconsin, he had said Dolly Castle had taken the study-abroad program to Shatrunjaya Hills, India.

The mystery was solved!

Brando, who for all I knew had a hand in creating the Ronald McDonald statues Dolly had vandalized, had built a statue that had injured innocent bystanders. Dolly, swept up in the cause of the unfairly injured Jains, was doling out her own form of weird punishment by stealing his statues. I wondered if her group, PEAS, even existed or was just a front for her as she skulked around Battle Lake and Alexandria, publicly humiliating Brando while he was in town to celebrate a Wenonga-less Chief Wenonga Days.

It was time to confront one Dolly Castle, woman to woman.

TWENTY-FIVE

Mrs. Berns was only too happy to open and run the library by herself. "Kennie and I need to meet, anyhow."

That stopped me cold. "What're you and Kennie meeting about?" The two normally didn't get along well, except when they believed a profit was at stake. Their last joint venture was old-lady beauty contests, which had developed a strong niche market but never took off like they had dreamed. I didn't want them to be dreaming their sordid entrepreneurial dreams in my library.

She shuffled away from me. "Never you mind."

I followed her. "Are you two going to start another business?"

"We're just going to hang out and talk."

"But you don't like Kennie."

Mrs. Berns cackled. "I didn't like my last husband, either, but that didn't stop me from enjoying his company, if you know what I mean. Now stop worrying and go save your boy."

"OK, but remember, if anything happens to the library, we're both out of work."

She gave me a curt German "Ach!" and sent me on my way. My first stop was the Battle Lake Motel, where I was grateful to see Dolly's black Honda still parked. The rain must have kept her inside. I pulled my car into Halvorson Park and debated whether to knock on her door and just straight up ask her what was going on or to hide in the rain and follow her when she finally left. I decided on subterfuge, and settled in for a wait. About forty-five minutes passed, and the inside of my windshield was becoming foggy. It was raining too hard to leave the windows down, so I started my car and turned on the defrost. I fiddled with my knob until I tuned in 92.3, the classic rock station out of Alexandria. Led Zeppelin's "When the Levee Breaks" blues-rocked over the airwaves, and I took it as a good sign.

Shortly after that, I saw the doorknob on room number 7 jiggle, and Dolly's head popped out and then back in. When she emerged a minute later, she carried an aqua-blue umbrella. She dashed through the downpour into her car, too engrossed in staying dry to notice if she was being watched or followed.

When Dolly pulled out and drove past Halvorson Park, I let one car slip between us before following. As far as I knew, she didn't know what my car looked like, but better safe than sorry. She was heading through town, and the traffic was light, likely due to the storm. She stopped at the intersection of 78 and 210, and kept driving south on 78. When she turned east shortly after 78 briefly divided into double-lane, I wondered where she was headed. If she was returning to Wisconsin, this wasn't the quickest way to 94. This back road offered only a Bible camp, Inspiration Peak, and farms.

I turned left to follow Dolly, and my radio lost its signal. I fiddled with static before the entire mechanism bopped out and began screeching. This happened often in my little Toyota, particularly when it rained. I punched the volume button off and sniffed in the wet green of the Minnesota grassland jungle. To the south of the road was a herd of wet and grazing buffalo, and to the north were rolling hills dotted with sumac and prairie grass. The bucolic scenery was all covered in sheets of wet gray, the rain falling so fast that it ran downhill instead of being absorbed by the parched ground.

I was getting relaxed following Dolly, and suddenly, as I crested the last hill before the Peak, the supper club nestled at the base of Inspiration Peak, she was out of sight. She must have turned left on the gravel road right before the Peak because the blacktop road stretched straight and curving to the right was empty. I pulled into the dinner club's parking lot and considered my options. If I followed the gravel, I could either drive straight, past farmhouses, or turn right, up to the Inspiration Peak parking lot.

I had been to Inspiration Peak a few times before, mostly in the fall when the leaves were a blazing quilt of reds, golds, and oranges. At 1,750 feet, about 400 feet above the surrounding landscape, Inspiration Peak was the highest point in Otter Tail County and the third highest point in all of Minnesota. The rumor was that Sinclair Lewis wrote some of his social criticism there, and that he had named this highest summit in the glacially carved Leaf Hills. It was a gut-busting straight-up hike to the top of the Peak but worth every ragged breath. You could see nearly thirty miles in every direction on a clear day.

Was it possible Dolly was just out here for some sightseeing and hiking? Unlikely, given the rain. Still, I might as well check out the dead-end parking lot at the base of the Peak so I could rule out her having taken that route. I swung a right, heading up the paved driveway, and wasn't surprised that the parking lot was empty. I looped around to head back down the hill when a darker shape in the woods off to my right caught my eye. I rolled down my window and squinted through the rain, making out what appeared to be a hatchback pulled up off the road and under an enormous sheltering pine. It was Dolly's car. What was she doing at Inspiration Peak during a rain shower?

Shit. I was going to have to get out and see what was up. In the spirit of staying undercover, I drove my car the half mile to the Peak Supper Club's deserted parking lot, left my Toyota behind the dumpster, grabbed my flashlight, and dragged my miserable butt out into the rain. The downpour had tapered off to a steady shower, and at least it was warm, but it's never fun to be wet in clothes. At least Dolly would be easy to follow in the mud, I consoled myself glumly as I sloshed along. I backtracked to her car and was unsurprised to find it empty. Fresh hiking boot tracks, filling up softly with rain under the protection of the hardwoods, led off trail and into the woods.

The oaks and pine kept the worst of the rain off of me, but the musty smell of wet leaves and pine needles clung to me. It wasn't long before I felt a crawling sensation at the back of my neck—a woodtick, looking for room and board. I pulled it out of my shirt and squished its rubbery body with my thumbnail before flinging it into the woods. It was all over now. I had woodtick fever, head to toe, inside and out. Every branch brushing against my skin, every raindrop trickling down my naked arm, every tingle in my scalp was a hungry woodtick looking to plunge its fangs into my flesh and grow corpulent, blue-gray and lethargic, like a vampiric blueberry dangling from my defenseless body. Ugh. I was so caught up in my paranoia that I didn't notice the yellow sign warning me that I was leaving state park grounds.

I also didn't notice that the landscape was changing from hardwoods and some pine, to pine and some scrub, to marsh fern and fringed loosestrife—native swamp plants. I was heading into uncertain ground, and it wasn't until my feet made a sucking noise as I pulled them up for a step that I truly looked around. Dolly's hiking boot trail was still in front of me, though harder to follow now that the trees were no longer protecting it from the rain. And I was definitely entering a swamp. I could tell by the lay of the land and by the boggy, canned-fish smell in the air. Behind me was the Inspiration Peak parking lot, now nearly a mile back. In front of me was my one chance to free Johnny. I had no choice but to continue, and to add leech fever to my list of worries.

The rain was finally easing off, and I cocked my ear to listen for any sign of Dolly stopping or backtracking on me. Nothing but the soft sound of rain and some far-off thunder. I plodded gingerly forward, putting my sandal-shod feet on fallen sticks where possible and sinking into the muck where it wasn't. I took solace in the fact that Dolly didn't seem to be having any better time of it than me, judging by her footprints. A half-mile later, I was through the swamp and back into the relative comfort of emerald-green prairie grass and shoulder-height red sumac. That is where I lost the trail.

I searched frantically, starting at the last footprint and working outward in concentric circles. When I started hitting the swamp again on the far side of the circle, I began to worry. I strode away from the swamp and to the highest hill in front of me, careful to stick close to the ground and make as little noise as possible. From my poor excuse for a perch, I could see an abandoned farmstead in front of me and Inspiration Peak looming behind me. I didn't see any movement in the farmstead, but it was worth a look-see since I had come this far.

I made my way carefully toward the sagging barn, its red paint faded to a rusty brown. The back of the barn was facing me, a tired silo on one side and on the other, an abandoned farmhouse, its front windows years ago shattered by some teens, undoubtedly, or maybe a drunken Sinclair Lewis. Some proud oaks surrounded the old structures, but here were no other buildings. A dirt road, churned up and hazardous from the rain, led away from the buildings. From this distance, I couldn't tell if the road had been used recently.

I was near the abandoned farmstead, sticking close to the ground and behind sumac shrubs, when I spotted movement. It was Dolly, leaving the house. The entry was doorless, so she simply walked through the opening and toward the barn. She strode briskly, confidently, not like she was exploring but rather like she was finishing up business.

I studied the short distance between the barn and me. The only cover left was prairie grass, but thankfully, there were no windows on the backside. As if on jungle patrol, I made a quiet dash toward the barn and reached the rear without seeing anyone else move. I dropped to all fours, my bare knees soaking up mud and moisture from the drenched ground, and crawled to the side of the building. I couldn't hear any human movement, and so I hugged the ground tighter and wormed my way along the side, meaning to peek at the front.

I continued, unmolested, until I made out the soft murmurings of voices. I couldn't hear what they were saying, but it was clearly a man and a woman talking, and they sounded angry. I risked poking my head around the front and saw that the entire face of the barn was exposed, the sliding door having fallen or been taken off its roller long ago. I noticed that second. What I noticed first was the two huge, sandal-clad feet sticking out of the front of the barn. Twenty-eight-foot, fiberglass-Norse-warrior big.

TWENTY-SIX

It was Big Ole, and he was in four pieces. Did Dolly have Chief Wenonga here, too? I tried to peek around at the silo, hoping to spy a shock of black hair poking over the top that I had maybe missed before. I didn't get my head too far before Dolly came storming out, followed by Les.

"We agreed on $2,500," Les was saying gruffly. I hadn't gotten a good look at him before I ducked back around the corner, but I could hear rage in his voice.

"I said I'd pay you $2,500 in exchange for two very specific things. You've only delivered one."

"One big one! Not one person saw me or my brother leave with that statue. That's worth $2,500 alone!"

I bet Dolly was going to say something really important then, something like, "But you messed up getting Chief Wenonga and forced me to murder Liam Anderson, so you're only getting $1,250 and be lucky you're getting anything, and I never even kissed Johnny Leeson because he said he loves Mira James who's for sure way better in bed than I could ever be," but I would never know because at that unfortunate moment, a crow squawked behind me. An evil, murderous squawk that would have scared any normal human being out of her skin. I jumped out and landed plop on the ground near Dolly and Les. They both looked at me like I had just fallen out of a cow's behind.

"Hi." That's all I could get out before Les lunged at me, loaded for bear. He had munitions strapped across his chest in an "X," a knife belt around each skinny thigh, a stun gun at his hip (why hadn't I brought my own blessed stun gun?), and a sword in a scabbard at his back. He landed on top of me and quickly spun my arms and his legs around in circles, twisting my body in some elaborate half-nelson-crossface-chickenwing arm lock, accompanied by high-pitched Bruce Lee karate sounds. When he had wrestled me into an ungainly position, confident that I could not move, he demanded, "How do you like that, missy?"

Too bad Les was not a gifted wrestler. He mostly had himself tangled and me by the wrists. A flick of each, and I stood up and he fell harmlessly off of me. "It was kind of gross, Les. So, you stole Big Ole?"

Air escaped Dolly in a frustrated whoof. "Jesus, Les. What was that? I thought you were going to hurt her. You need to be more careful."

I eyeballed Dolly. "You don't want him to hurt me? I could spill the beans about all this." I waved my arm to encompass the sandaled feet and generous thighs of Big Ole, lying on his back in the shade of the barn. I also glanced quickly up his skirt—neuter, I knew it—but I think my peek was suave enough that Dolly didn't notice.

"I don't want anyone hurt. I never did."

"Especially the Jains?"

Dolly's sea-green eyes narrowed. She was mud-up-to-her-knees, her sodden strawberry blonde hair was escaping her ponytail and plastering itself to her cheeks, and her hands were on her hips so tight I thought they might leave bruises. "Especially the Jains. You know about the statue in India?"

"I only have theories. The one thing I can tell you for sure, though, is that Johnny Leeson is in jail for something he didn't do."

"What?"

"Johnny was arrested yesterday. A dead body was found at his cabin on Silver Lake, some guy from Wisconsin named Liam Anderson. Sound familiar?"

"No." Dolly said this with genuine surprise in her voice, followed by a wave of concern on her face. "They think Johnny killed him?"

"They do. And this Liam Anderson is missing a chunk of his scalp, a chunk that matches the hairy mess found at the base of Chief Wenonga's statue. Whoever killed Liam Anderson probably also stole the Chief, and it follows that whoever stole the Chief, also stole Big Ole."

"See!" Les exploded. "I told you we shouldn't take Ole so close to Wenonga disappearing! You said no one would connect the two, that the police wouldn't be involved. Crazy woman. Crazy Indian-lovin' woman."

"Calm down."

"You two took Ole, but not Wenonga?" That would be like breaking into a chocolate store and only taking the money. "Dolly, you know Les has been following you since you got to town, don't you?"

Dolly's hands left her hips and hung at her sides. She suddenly looked very, very tired. "Not me. Brando. I hired him to follow Brando and get enough information to pin the Chief's disappearance on him." At this point, she glared at Les. "He didn't get me anything."

This was why Les hadn't earned his full $2,500—he had snatched Big Ole but hadn't dug up any information on Brando. It made sense. The two times I had seen Les skulking around in the shadows, I had assumed he was following Dolly, but Brando was at both locations both times. "Why do you think Brando stole Wenonga?"

"Not think. Know." Dolly shook her head with resignation, swiping her hair off her face and tucking it back into her ponytail. A reluctant smile played at the corners of her generous mouth. "You're quite the snoop, you know that?"

I shook my head. "I prefer to think of myself as curious. Johnny isn't really involved in this, is he? If you tell me what's going on, I can help to get him out of jail."

Dolly appeared to weigh her options before she began talking. Her speech was fast, too fast to take notes if we had been in class. "I was in Shatrunjaya Hills, India, last semester, leading a study abroad class. While there, I got involved with a group fighting the corporate invasion of the country. McDonald's was the obvious face of this rampant capitalism, and that's where we concentrated our energies. It was small-time civil disobedience at first—cutting off the arms of Ronald McDonald, spray-painting anticorporate messages on the side of the corporate offices, staging protests outside the front doors of the restaurant while dressed as mad cows.

"Then, someone in our group blew up a McDonald's. No one was hurt, but I realized that it had gone too far. I packed up and was getting ready to leave when I heard about the Gandhi statue. I had been passing it every day on my way to class, and one day, it just fell over. It hurt some people, Jains on their pilgrimage, but it seemed like an accident. That is, until a local investigation revealed that the statue was structurally unsound. It was only a matter of time until it fell. That's when Brando flew onto the scene, greasing palms and swishing away with the evidence before any charges could be pressed. The insurance claims would have put him under."

"Did you and he meet there?"

"No. And it was just coincidence I ended up hired in Stevens Point, where Fibertastic Enterprises is housed. But once that fell in my lap, I knew it was karma. It was up to me to right the wrongs that had been done by Brando Erikkson's company in India. I just didn't know how, at first."

I shook my head knowingly. "And you came up with the plan to humiliate Brando by stealing his statues?"

"Humiliate him? Wouldn't that be rather childish? No, after researching, I found out that the Gandhi statue, the Big Ole statue, and the Chief Wenonga statue were all made from the same mold. It followed that all three had the same structural deficiencies, and if I could prove that, I could prove that the Gandhi statue falling wasn't an accident. Brando would be forced to pay up."

"Huhn?" Her car had passed mine about two sentences back. "How could they all three be made from the same mold? Big Ole is at least five feet taller than Chief Wenonga."

"It's all in the legs, sweetie. See for yourself."

She led me back to Big Ole and showed me where extra length had been added to his calves and thighs. I had always thought it was the skirt that made his legs look unnaturally long, but it had been part of the design. I remembered Brando telling me in the coffee shop that oftentimes in his business one mold was reused, with minor design changes to differentiate one statue from another. And that explained the strange familiarity I had felt when looking at pictures of the Big Ole and Mahatma Gandhi statues. They were Wenonga's brothers, man. "So why did you steal Big Ole? Why not just get some engineer to check him out?"

"That was the original plan, to get an engineering professor from UW–Stevens Point to examine Chief Wenonga. Then he was stolen. I had a hunch it was Brando, and if I let him get Big Ole, there would go any chance of me connecting him to the crime in India. So, I quickly rearranged my plans and paid Mr. Militia here to borrow Big Ole for me until the professor could come and check him out. He's supposed to meet me here today."

I felt dizzy and realized I still had my hand on Big Ole's thigh. So much information to digest. I went back to the beginning. "You said you think Brando stole Chief Wenonga."

"I know he did. I just don't know how to prove it. My best guess is that this Liam Anderson was helping him, but that he has no traceable connections to Brando, and was the only witness to Brando's plan. That man is devious."

I agreed. I was falling for her story, lock, stock, and barrel, when a realization slapped me across the face like an angry girl. "You slept with Brando. I saw him leaving your motel room the night before last. Les saw it too."

Dolly's cheeks reddened. "I was desperate for information. I figured it'd be easier to sleep with him and find out what he knew than steal Big Ole out of Alexandria. I ended up having to do both."

There, but for the grace of God, go I. I could hardly judge the woman, given the loin-rubbing I had done with Brando last night. Speaking of…I couldn't help myself. "Was he good?"

Dolly nodded ruefully, her green eyes bright with memory. "I'm sorry to say he was fantastic. A truly delicious lover."

Fuckin' A.

"But watch out. He seems stupid and pretty, but he's dangerous. Vindictive, and smart as a snake. Good luck connecting him to any of this. That's why I had to steal Big Ole. I don't know how you're going to get Johnny out of jail."

"Dolly?"

"Yeah?"

"Did you sleep with Johnny, too?"

At this, she laughed. "I wish. No, all he wanted to do was talk about Stevens Point and my teaching. At first, I was flattered, but then it got kind of boring."

"So why did you go to his cabin?"

"How'd you know I was out at his cabin?" Dolly eyed Les suspiciously, maybe wondering if he was working both sides.

"I saw you leaving," I lied.

"Saturday night, after the fireworks? Yeah, I thought I would give it one last shot. Figured I'd try the old, 'sneak into his bed' trick. When I got there, though, the door looked broken in and Johnny's car was gone. I left."

That old "sneak into his bed" trick. I could scarcely talk to a man I had a crush on, let alone sneak into his bed. You'd think a quality like that would have bred itself out over a generation or two, but here I was. "Saturday night was the only night you were there?"

"Yes. I haven't seen Johnny since."

That squared with what I knew. Johnny said he had left town after the fireworks, and there would have been no reason for him to go back to his cabin before he did. "What if I just go to the police and tell them what you told me about the statue?"

"I intend to go myself, as soon as my colleague comes to examine Big Ole. I'll nail Brando for India, that I'm sure of. As far as connecting him to Wenonga and dead Mr. Anderson, I'm afraid that will only ever be speculation, unless you get some divine inspiration. Brando is thorough, he's smart, and he doesn't leave a trail."

That wasn't good enough. I needed to get Johnny out of jail, the sooner the better. "When's your engineering professor coming?"

"Within the hour. He's got a Jeep, so he should be able to drive instead of walk. You're welcome to stay and see what he finds."

"No, I need to find some way to tie all this to Brando. Let me know when he gets busted for the Gandhi statue, though, won't you? I'd love to be there."

Dolly winked at me. "It's a date."

I trudged back the way I came, smarter but no happier. Even the rainbow that I glimpsed through the tops of the glistening pine trees did nothing to lift my spirits. When I made it back to my car, I was hot, wet, and dotted with mosquito bites. I motored back to Battle Lake, so lost in my internal dark cloud that I didn't notice I was on a strange gravel road. I decided to keep going forward—all gravel in Minnesota leads to blacktop eventually—and that's how I happened upon the enormous Virgin Mary on the side of the road.

It was another statue, twenty or so feet tall, and it had a sign in front that read "Our Lady of the Hills." I parked my car at the side of the road and got out, half-perturbed (how many frickin' gigantic statues does one county need?) and half-enraptured. The statue was beautiful. Her face was peaceful, and her straight brown hair and long blue robes blended nicely with the green pines she was tucked among. I walked closer and reached a locked box for offerings. This I passed and continued to her feet.

The statue was gazing out at a far-off place where there were answers. I pulled myself up onto her base, careful not to disturb her space, and stood on my tippy-toes to look inside her cupped hands. They were full of water from the rain, but in the palms and dripping down the fingers was a red liquid, as if her hands were bleeding. And that's when I knew how I would nail Brando. Divine inspiration, indeed.

TWENTY-SEVEN

I SPED INTO TOWN with one thought on my mind: I had to find Brando's vehicle, the embarrassingly oversized red Humvee. Brando had told me he was leaving town today, but I had a hunch that the missing Big Ole situation was going to keep him around for a little longer than he had originally planned. Our Lady of the Hills had shown me how to connect Brando to Liam Anderson's corpse, but he had to be around for me to do it.

My Toyota was pushing seventy as I crested the divided road hill heading into Battle Lake. I was too antsy to fiddle with my radio so tried to relax by concentrating on the day. The sky was clearing and the air smelled fresh, clean, and sauna hot. The moisture on the road was starting to evaporate, leaving sluggish worms to fend for themselves. I tried to drive around as many as I could, but the highway was flush with them.

I knew my first stop should be the cabin Brando had stayed at north of town to see if he had extended his stay. I didn't know exactly where north of town, but a little inquiring at the Fortune

Café told me that he was staying at Nifty Nook Resort on Otter Tail Lake. I buzzed out there and had his cabin pointed out to me by the friendly owners, who I knew from working at the library. They said he had indeed extended his stay but didn't think he was around at the moment.

I walked over to the cabin to be sure. Brando's Humvee wasn't in sight and a quick peek in the building's windows showed me an immaculate if small interior. The kitchen was spotless, with daisy-strewn curtains cutting the sunlight. The main room had a couch, a television, a game table, and a bookshelf, and the bedroom had a bed so tightly made, the spread looked like a tourniquet. My guess was that Brando had been so successful at bed-hopping in Battle Lake that he had never used this cabin.

I listened to the water of Otter Tail Lake lapping onto the sandy beach and considered my next move. Probably, I'd go back to town and ask around to see if anyone had seen Brando. If nothing else, Gina always had her ear to the ground and might be able to tell me whose legs and bed he had ended up in last night. I decided a quick cruise through the back streets of Battle Lake would be a good place to start before going door to door. There were really only seven avenues off of Lake Street anyhow. It was at the third street, in front of Kennie's house, that I stumbled across the parked Humvee. That woman certainly was taking her job as mayor and official welcomer seriously.

I parked my car, scarcely able to contain my excitement, and ran over to the Hummer. It didn't take long crouched down on my hands and knees to find exactly what I was looking for—red paint splashed onto all four wheel wells. The Virgin Mary's stigmata had made me think of it. I hadn't noticed the paint yesterday because of the Humvee's matching color. So it was Brando who had originally broken the balloons when he had gone on Saturday night to drop Liam Anderson's dead or dying body into what he assumed were empty cabins. It was Johnny's poor luck that he had chosen his.

Dolly was surely right that Brando hired Liam Anderson to help him remove the statue, and he must have slipped or something dropped on him in the process and he was hurt. Brando, apparently not one to be too troubled by his heart or conscience, didn't bring Anderson to the hospital. He must have been scouting out a hiding place to unload his hireling when he stumbled across Johnny's cabin. It wasn't teenagers who had been out there spinning shitties on Friday; it was Brando looking for a place to stash the dying man.

What he hadn't planned for was the paint-filled balloons Johnny had secreted under the pile of leaves at the head of the driveway. I had been too fixated on Dolly as the criminal to even check Brando's car before today. Now, I had hard evidence to bring to Gary Wohnt. I could prove that Brando had been to the cabin Saturday night, and that would be enough to launch an investigation.

"See anything you like?"

I stood so fast that I scraped my head on the wheel well. I whirled on Brando. "Not so much. Paying a house call to Kennie?"

"Something like that. What were you doing down there?"

I rubbed the tender spot on my noggin and pulled my hand away. Blood. How ironic. This man was good at separating people from parts of their head. "I dropped a bracelet."

Brando leaned into me, oozing sexuality and charm. "I've never seen you wear a bracelet." He circled my wrist with his large hand and caressed it. "You've got beautiful wrists."

"Thank you. I—" Before I could make my goodbyes, Brando clamped down on my arm and twisted it around and back, forcing me to turn my back to him to keep it from snapping. The pain sent hot mercury streaks up my arm and into my brain.

"I think we need to go for a ride. You'll like riding in the Humvee. You feel on top of the world."

His left hand opened the driver's side door as his right hand held me effortlessly. He gave my arm an extra twist, and I felt more than heard a pop. My knees buckled and he shoved me up and forward. My arm felt attached to my body by only one stretched sinew and to do anything but go forward would have snapped it free. I had one leg in the car when I spotted the rust-colored stains peeking out under a towel spread on the seat and carpeting.

He caught my gaze. "Time to get this reupholstered, don't you think? That's for tomorrow. I have a good friend who owes me a favor. For today, I think we'll just take a little joy ride."

Tears started spilling down my face despite myself. His grip was too tight to allow me to turn and look up and down the street, but I knew there had been no one outside when I pulled up, and it was too much to hope that Kennie would come out and save me. I couldn't fight or yell now without losing my arm, but he'd need to let go to drive, and then I would kick, scratch, and yell like a banshee.

Brando pushed me all the way across the driver's seat and gave a tiny yelp, which I mistook for sick glee. The pressure eased off my arm as quickly as it had come, and the lack of pain was exquisite. My arm hung limply at my side, not broken but not right, either. I turned to kick and run but was stopped short.

Brando was on his knees in an awkward genuflection, his face resting on the pavement. Mrs. Berns was behind him, crouched down, with one hand between his legs like a cocky quarterback taking the ball from her center. She winked at me. "I took a class on women's self-defense. What you do, you make a little crook, like so, with your thumb and forefinger and come up from behind and through the legs." She demonstrated with her free hand. "You squeeze that crook around the very top of the sac like you're castrating a pig, pinch, and twist until you can't twist no more. That way, you really get their attention."

Or you could, if they were conscious, I thought to myself. And who was running the library?

TWENTY-EIGHT

IT TOOK THREE DAYS and a couple search warrants to find out I had been mostly right about Brando and Liam Anderson. Brando had hired Liam for muscle to help him remove the statue, and according to Brando, Liam had slipped and fell once the statue had been removed. He scraped his head on the post on the way down. In Minnesota, there is no law requiring someone to bring another person to the hospital, no matter how dire their straits, so the death of Liam Anderson was ruled an accident, and no charges were filed.

However, Dolly's engineering friend found a structural flaw in Big Ole that would have resulted in him crushing some unsuspecting Lutherans with cameras in under a year if it hadn't been fixed. Which it was. It required trimming thirteen inches of thigh off the big guy, but he looked better for it, and now, he's as safe as Sesame Street. Finding the flaw in Ole had been enough to grant a search warrant for Fibertastic Enterprises, where the dismantled Gandhi was found stowed in a back storeroom. Apparently, Brando had been intending to resell the upper torso to a mini golf course in Branson, Missouri. There was enough left to prove that the same structural flaw that had threatened Big Ole had also sent the Gandhi statue tumbling in India, and Brando was forced to pay big to the Jains. His name and photo were on the cover of every newspaper in the Midwest, so he was humiliated as well as financially ruined.

That's not even the best news, though. They found my man. Brando had parked his Humvee with the dead or dying Liam in it in the woods near Johnny's cabin and driven the tractor trailer with Chief Wenonga in it all the way back to Stevens Point. There, it had been unloaded, and Brando had left instructions to have Wenonga's body spray-painted white, his hair spray-painted blonde, his eyes blue, his leather pants replaced with a half-robe, and the tomahawk replaced with a cross. You got it. My emotionally distant hunka hunka burning love had been this close to being reincarnated as a fiberglass Jesus. Thank god for miracles.

Speaking of miracles, it was at the Return of the Chief party that Mrs. Berns explained how she miraculously came to be outside of Kennie's house just in time to save me.

"Oh, that? Well, the library was kinda slow, and Kennie said she had a business proposition for me, so I locked 'er up and headed over."

I wiggled the fingers sticking out of my sling. The doctor said my arm was just strained and had given me a sling and prescribed some truly worthwhile painkillers. They were even better than Nyquil. I wasn't so medicated that I had lost all sense, however. I debated whether or not Mrs. Berns' work ethic and/or her business venture with Kennie were topics worth pursuing. "Yeah?"

"Yeah. I think the woman's really got something this time, too. She wants to run an online business with me."

My shoulders relaxed marginally. "Oh, that's great! Online businesses are really taking off. You have a wider market that way."

"It's going to be called 'Come Again.' We're going to sell previously owned and gently used marital aids. Kennie says it's an untapped market, what with the cost of some of those things new. And you break up with someone or get divorced, you don't want that stuff lying around to remind you what you had."

Technically, all true. "It sure is a beautiful day to get Wenonga back."

Brando's brother, Peter Erikkson, was now in charge of what was left of Fibertastic and had promised to work around the clock to get a repainted Chief Wenonga back to Halvorson Park by the weekend. He was true to his word. Kennie had arranged for the Battle Lake Bulldogs marching band to be present at the reinstallation of the statue. They had originally wanted to play "Apache," but Dolly, the town's honorary Historical Consultant and head of the new Diversity Advisory Panel, had suggested they play something less culturally weighted, hence "Wipe Out."

In the shortest town meeting in history, the Advisory Panel had decided that Chief Wenonga and Chief Wenonga Days were here to stay, but the celebration would from here on out be a true celebration of the First Nation people as well as the immigrants who had since arrived. That might still include turtle races, a street dance, and all-town garage sale, but it would also include historical tours through Glendalough, no more stereotypical representations of Native Americans in the parade, and introspective pieces in the *Recall*. There was even talk of changing the name of Wenonga Days to the Heritage Festival.

Change can be good, I thought, shading my eyes against the late afternoon sun that was reflecting gloriously off the ebony hair of Chief Wenonga. There were at least two hundred people in Halvorson Park doing the same, many of them tourists. Business was booming in town, thanks to the nationwide publicity Wenonga's and Ole's disappearances had brought. I looked around for Sid or Nancy, knowing one of them would be here. I felt a hand tap my shoulder.

"Mira?"

It was Johnny, still tanned, rippling, and smelling of vanilla and warm earth, despite his two days in the clink. Other than the tired pull around his eyes and his hesitant smile, he seemed to be my old Johnny. I smiled at him. "You look so hot."

"What?"

"You look shot. That's what I said. It's something we used to say in Paynesville. You know, like 'you look kind of tired.' Guess that saying didn't make it over to Wisconsin." I giggled a tad hysterically and fought the urge to pull out my painkillers and convince him I had a prescription to be stupid.

"No, I guess it didn't." He rubbed his hands across the front of his jeans, glanced in my eyes and looked hastily away. "I heard you helped bring the Chief back."

"No, that was all Dolly. You were right to check her out, you know. She had all the information. She just didn't know who to share it with."

"I thought she stole the Chief."

"Yeah, me too."

"Mira?" This time he held my gaze. His eyes were a deeper blue than I had ever seen them, and I had to struggle not to look away. "I heard you helped me get out of jail."

"Oh, that would have happened sooner or later."

He reached for my arm, looked angrily at my sling, and pulled back. "You trusted me, and that means something to me."

It was too much. I was going to cry or hump his leg, neither of which I wanted accompanied by "Wipe Out" and an audience of two hundred. I twisted to lose myself in the crowd, but not before he grabbed my good hand.

"Wait." I turned back and thought I saw a kiss in his eyes before he looked away shyly. "I owe you a thank you."

I nodded, wondering why my fight-or-flight mechanism was kicking in. Johnny wanted to thank me, and if I let it, it could be the best thank you ever, much better than a card. That's when his cell phone vibrated against his hip.

He reluctantly reached for it and got a worried look when he saw the number. "It's my mom. I have to take it."

He stepped away, leaving me vibrating without the need for electricity. Was this my chance to fall for a good guy? I couldn't concentrate on what he was saying, but when he turned back to me, the concerned look was on his face for a different reason. "I'm sorry, I have to go. My mom hasn't seen me since I got out of jail, and I need to show her I'm all right."

My disappointment was palpable, but how upset can you be with a guy who worries about his mom? "That's OK. I appreciate the thank you."

He pushed a stray hair off my cheek. "I can come over tonight. Will you be around?"

Do Norwegians like white food? "I think so."

"I'll knock three times." He smiled his shy grin and walked away.

TWENTY-NINE

I HURRIED HOME TO get shaved and perfumed—no beer and eggs in my hair this time—and was ready like a rocket for him. If I was going to do this, I was going to do it 100 percent. It went without saying that this was my last shot at a healthy relationship, of course. If it didn't work with Johnny, it was the nunnery—or a quick trip back to the Cities to finish my grad program and become a dried up, cat-collecting, fist-shaking, asexual English professor. I had pulled Dr. Lindstrom's note back out after I had arrived home from the Return of the Chief party:

> Dear Mira:
> You are missed! I hope you haven't gotten so involved in the active animal rights movement up there in God's country that you can't give us a hand back here. I need a research assistant this fall, and you're my woman. Pay is meager, but your tuition would be free. Is it a deal? Respond at your convenience, as long as it is before August.
> Sincerely yours, Dr. Michael Lindstrom

Smoothing the note on my counter top, I made a deal with myself. If Johnny came tonight, I would give him a chance. I would open up to him in every way I could. If he didn't show, or he came and turned out to be like every other guy I had ever been with except for Jeff, I was packing it up and moving back to the Cities. No one could say I hadn't given Battle Lake a chance. But oh, did I hope that Johnny would do right by me tonight.

I tried to read and watch TV but spent most of the time squirming and beaming at my animals. Johnny Leeson was going to be with me tonight. I watched anxiously for the telltale head-lights down the driveway, the clock ticking a happy beat. The beat, however, soon became monotonous, and then taunting. At first, I consoled myself by pointing out that Johnny had just said "to-night," and not given a specific time. Then, I moved on to worry-ing. Johnny was a decent guy, and he would have called to cancel if he could have. By 11 PM, however, I had decided that Johnny had had second thoughts. Fine. That's fine. It probably would have had a terrible ending anyhow, with me finding out he was a lousy lover, or emotionally distant and unable to commit to a relation-ship even though we both really liked each other and had buckets in common, or a collector of toenail clippings.

That's what I was telling myself as I walked past my front door, angrily ripping off the cute T-shirt I had chosen just for the occa-sion, the one that actually made me look like I had boobs. When, I wondered fiercely, would relationships with men stop being pain-ful experiences I had to learn from and instead be a nurturing re-lationship I could grow in? Never. Absolutely never. I rubbed hot tears out of the corner of my eyes, angry at myself for even getting my hopes up. It was the cloister for me, or maybe a job teaching English at a rural technical college.

That's when the first knock came. I jumped back from the door and pulled my T-shirt back on. I hadn't heard or seen a car. Then the second knock came, and my heart and loins did a little leprechaun kick. What was on the other side of this door was going to decide whether I returned to the U of M to be Dr. Michael Lindstrom's research assistant or whether I stayed in Battle Lake a little longer.

Instead of waiting for the third knock, I ripped open the door, naked hope in my eyes. The hope quickly turned to shock, and then confusion. Actually, I shouldn't have been surprised at the body before me. This was Battle Lake, after all. Anything can happen here, and it usually does.

BOOK CLUB QUESTIONS

1. Red herrings in mysteries are clues that lead the reader astray. Which red herrings did you notice in *Knee High by the Fourth of July*, and which were most effective?

2. Battle Lake is a real town in Minnesota. In what ways can you relate to this setting, and how does it move the story forward?

3. How central is the setting to the book's plot and character?

4. In what way does Dr. Dolly Castle serve as a "foil" for Mira? In what way is she a "double"?

5. Mira James is independent, not afraid of her sexuality, and willing to speak her mind. How would the series be different if she were in a relationship, or shy, or less colorful in her language? Would a relationship with Johnny Leeson change the tone of the book?

6. Similarly, Mira is plagued by her past, as many people are. How do her past trials, traumas, and tragedies influence her actions in her current adventures?

7. Consider the contemporary female protagonists in mystery: Stephanie Plum, Kinsey Millhone, Tess Monaghan, etc. What makes for a lasting female protagonist?

8. On a related note, how does Mira James compare with other female sleuths? What makes her different? How does she resemble

some of the most popular and beloved female protagonists in mystery?

9. The Murder-by-Month books have been categorized as everything from amateur sleuth mysteries (mysteries with a reluctant yet plucky "everywoman" at the center of the action; authors who write in this genre include Diane Mott Davidson, Carolyn Hart, and Susan Wittig Albert) to cozies (lighter mysteries with no graphic sex or violence and often a small-town setting; think Rochelle Krich, Mary Higgins Clark, and Julia Buckley) to humorous or comic caper mysteries (whimsical mysteries where laughing goes hand in hand with solving the crime; Carl Hiaasen, Janet Evanovich, and Parnell Hall all fall in this category). Which of these three categories would you put the Murder-by-Month Mysteries into, and why?

10. Although the central mystery of *Knee High by the Fourth of July* is wrapped up at the end of the book, another mystery begins. Who would you like to see at Mira's door? Who do you think is actually at Mira's door, and what are the repercussions of this?

If you enjoyed *Knee High by the Fourth of July,* read on for an excerpt from the next Murder-by-Month Mystery by Jess Lourey.

August Moon

COMING SOON FROM MIDNIGHT INK

AUGUST

August lumbered in, the weather grew impossibly hotter, and farmers muttered about drought as their crops turned crispy and their irrigation systems taxed the water supply. Those just visiting loved the hot, clear weather, and the beaches and local shops were packed like seeds in a pomegranate. The out-of-towners seemed not to notice the lawns turning brown or the watering bans, and happily packed themselves into Stub's every night to enjoy live music and juicy butterknife steaks. In this way, the dance between the needs of an agricultural community and the requirements of a tourist-based economy played out against each other as they had since rich East Coasters discovered the beauty, solitude, and plentiful fish in Battle Lake back in the early 1900s.

When a little downtime in the library presented itself, I created a banned books display to feed my low-burning but constant anger and frustration. The display featured some of my favorite books of all time. *Of Mice and Men, The Catcher in the Rye, I Know*

Why the Caged Bird Sings, A Wrinkle in Time, The Color Purple, pretty much anything by Judy Blume and Stephen King, the Harry Potter series, and *The Handmaid's Tale*. I took grim pleasure in the fact that the books flew off the display and I needed to continually dig for more censored literature to add.

Before I knew it, it was Friday, August 13, and it was time to interview the crop of hopefuls to find the new worker. Mrs. Berns had agreed to come in early with me to get the library spick and span before the interviews. Not surprisingly, I found myself alone in the yellow brick building at 8 AM on this scorched but cloudy day. The weather, a colicky mix of heat and shade, set my teeth on edge as I unlocked the library door. The air had a hint of smoke, despite the burning ban, which created a mental image of the prairies surrounding us going up like a Kleenex. When a rap came on the door behind me and pulled me out of my fatalistic thoughts, I was grateful. *Mrs. Berns*, I figured. *Now I'll have someone around to be mad at.*

I turned and was surprised to see a young and pretty woman instead of a geriatric and libidinous one. I made the universal, point-at-your-watch-and-shake-your-head gesture for "we're closed, come back later," but the woman shrugged her shoulders and smiled like she didn't understand.

I pulled the door open. "The library doesn't open up until 10:00. You'll have to come back in a coupla hours."

"Oh no! I've got a super-long shift, and I don't have a thing to read. I was supposed to be at work five minutes ago, but I can't bear the thought of another day without any books! I love those romances. I'm Alicia, by the way." She held out her manicured hand.

I knew Alicia, or at least her type. It was her brunette-Barbie beauty, youthful arrogance, and over-familiar, "you'll give me whatever I want, won't you?" smile that tipped me off. She was *that* girl, the one who, in middle school, got all the other desperate follower girls to wear their Guess jeans and turtle necks on Monday, and then showed up in a completely different outfit herself and made fun of them for being uncool. On Tuesday, she'd coach those same lonely girls to be mean to a randomly chosen chick in their group. When Wednesday rolled around, she'd make them all drink some nasty concoction to show their loyalty to her, and then ignore them when the popular kids strolled past. And so it went, until no girl in Alicia's orbit knew who she could trust and either got smart and started hanging out with the nerds or the druggies, or morphed into a miniature, poorly dressed Alicia. Be sure and ask me how I know so much about what the lonely follower girls went through in public school.

Yes, I knew Alicia's type, the ones who were pretty, popular, confident, and entitled in elementary, middle, and high school and thought they could coast on that for the rest of their life. Too bad no one bothered to tell them you could only cash those checks until you were eighteen. After that, the playing field evened out. A little. "Sorry. You'll have to come back later. Maybe over your lunch break?"

"Is that a mouse behind you?"

I turned toward where she was pointing. "I don't see anything."

"I swear I just saw something run under that desk over there. Maybe it was a rat. I'm gonna go peek, and we can herd it outside together." Alicia sailed past me, flashing a conspiratorial grin on the way. We were going to hunt rodents together. No scaredy cats, us.

She crouched on all fours. "Mind turning on the lights?"

I flipped the switch and went to fire up the front computer. There was no mouse, but she was going to entertain me in exchange for letting her in early. Crafty, that one, I thought as I appraised her. She was an inch or two taller than my five feet six, maybe ten pounds lighter but two cup sizes larger, and her long brown hair was curled and sprayed into place. She wore a fair amount of makeup, but it was expertly applied to look natural.

She was cute and she wanted to play Power Ball, but I wasn't in the mood. That was more telling than any other sad-sack thing I had done in the last four weeks. If I wasn't willing to outwit an obvious control freak in my own territory, I was seriously depressed. "If there was a mouse, it's long gone. You might as well grab a book or two since you're in here already."

"You sure you don't want me to get the mouse?"

"We both know there's no mouse. Do you need a library card, too?"

"If you don't mind."

I slid the form toward her. "Fill this out."

Alicia attempted to catch my eye and make nice, but I kept my gaze fixed on my computer screen. When she grabbed a pencil out of the cup in front of me and filled out the form, though, her necklace caught my eye. It was a delicate golden cross hugged tight around her neck, like a choker, and splayed on the cross was a tiny, crucified Jesus in all his scrawny glory.

She caught me staring. "It was a gift from my mom."

"Hmm. Where'd you say you work?"

"I didn't." She slid the card back toward me. Alicia Meale, and an address in Clitherall, the two-bars-and-a-post-office town just up the road from Battle Lake. Ms. Meale looked like she had neither done an honest day's work in her life nor eaten venison, pheasant, or snapping turtle, which would make her stand out like a purple pig in that town.

"You're new around here?"

"Not exactly. We've been here a few months. Anyhow, I better be going, or my boss is going to get crazy angry. It took longer to get a card than I thought it would. Maybe I'll come back over my lunch hour?"

"We're open until 5:00."

"Great! This is an awesome library." She trailed her fingers over the front counter as she left, and stopped at the banned-book display on her way out. "Unbelievable!" She laughed. "You've got a display of banned books! Too cool for school. Aren't you worried you're going to get in trouble?"

I warmed to her a hair, a microscopic, split-end of a hair. Maybe she was a misplanted chick, just like me. "In Battle Lake, you don't get in trouble. It gets in you. Besides, they're just books."

"You're a little bit of a rebel, Mira James."

The door dinged as she let herself out, and I looked around for anywhere my name would appear. I didn't wear a name tag, announce my name or station anywhere on the front desk, and I didn't post newsletters around town. For someone I had never met before, she knew a little too much for my comfort. Or maybe my depression was making me paranoid, as well.

I shelved the books that had been dropped after closing last night, dusted and vacuumed, and had all the resumés arranged by the time of the first interview when Mrs. Berns showed up.

"You're late."

"I'm here."

I blew air out my mouth and let the issue drop. The plan was for her to run the library as I conducted the interviews, but to check in on all the candidates surreptitiously. That was funny, because Mrs. Berns was subtle like a yeast infection. I figured, though, since she was going to work with whomever I hired, she had a right to weigh in on them.

"How many applicants have you got?" Today, Mrs. Berns was looking exactly like you'd think a little old lady should—tight-curled apricot hair, penciled-in eyebrows, big saggy nose shading a pair of salmon-pink lips, a red Sedona T-shirt one of her grand-kids had given her, a pair of white shorts, and white bootie socks with flat white tennies. If not for the pair of sharpshooters tucked into her gun belt, you'd want to hug her and call her Grandma.

"Four interviews, Mrs. Berns. What's up with the pistols?"

"These?" She tugged them out of their holsters and fired a couple rounds toward the ceiling. The smell of sulfur filled the air as the caps popped off. Delicate smoke curled out of each plastic barrel. "I had such a hoot with them and Bill after the Fourth of July parade that I figured I'd just hang on to them. They make a good conversation piece. Now tell me again why we're hiring someone else, chickenshit."

"If you promise to stop calling me chickenshit." It was how she had been addressing me since early July.

"No can do, Kemosabe."

I sighed. The door opened, saving me from a chickenshit reply. In walked a woman whose attitude was certainly in its fifties if she was not. Her gray-flecked hair was noosed back in a severe bun, her scraggly eyebrows shot out from her horn-rimmed, bechained glasses, and her nose spread out in an effort to slow its descent into the colorless razor-cut where her lips should be. Her blouse was gray, as was the sweater tied over her shoulders, the shapeless pencil skirt covering her bony lower body, and her support hose. The only flashes of color were her black, orthopedic shoes. She apparently had not gotten the memo that librarians were cool.

"You hire her, girl, and I'll make her life a living hell."

I believed Mrs. Berns, and I believed it when she said it before, during, and after the next two interviews, one with a statuesque former ballerina who could no longer dance due to a toe injury, and the other with a shiny-faced boy fresh out of grad school. The spitballs she lobbed at them along with the fake cat turd she pretended to slip on while I interviewed each ("Ouch, my hip!") cemented their lack of interest in the job. When the fourth woman walked in at noon, I was frazzled, frustrated, and not optimistic. This candidate looked like a brown-haired Shelley Long circa *Cheers*, with good posture and a bad perm, and in her early forties. She struck me as one of those women who was so pleasant and average as to be almost invisible. Her name was Sarah Ruth O'Hanlon, and according to her resumé, she had ten years' experience as an assistant librarian in the St. Cloud Regional Library system.

When she shook my hand, her grip was firm and dry. "Welcome to our library," I said. My eyes furtively scanned the room for Mrs. Berns, who had gone AWOL when she saw Sarah Ruth enter.

"Thank you. It's lovely, as is this town. I appreciate your time."

When Mrs. Berns leapt up behind the giant green dinosaur in the kids' reading section and popped a couple caps, followed by a hoot, a holler, and a thunderous fart, Sarah Ruth didn't flinch. "You're hired," I said.

"What?"

"Your resumé looks impeccable, and the job starts immediately. Are you interested?"

"Well, I, ah, I guess." She smiled at me, a little frown line between her eyes. "Are you sure you don't want to call my references?"

"Do you think you'd be okay living in Battle Lake?"

"I imagine so. I grew up in a small town, and I have family here." She nodded at me, convincing herself as she spoke. "I think I'd love it."

"That's all the reference I need." I smiled on the outside. "Can you start training on Monday?"

Sarah Ruth gripped my proffered hand warmly, and rested her free one over it. "I think you and I will get along great, Ms. James." I became aware of a tiny silver crucifix on her neck, a miniature version of the one Alicia Meale had been wearing this morning. Crosses were not unusual, but crucifixes were rarely worn as jewelry in these parts.

"That's an interesting necklace. Do you mind if I ask you where you got it?"

Her hands dropped and moved self-consciously to her throat. "It's a little macabre, don't you think? My niece bought it for me in Mexico, and I wear it out of loyalty. It wouldn't be my first choice in jewelry, given my druthers."

Mrs. Berns, who had holstered her pistols and army-crawled to the open spot in the middle of the library where I was conducting interviews, saved me from a reply. "Shit or get off the pot."

"Excuse me?"

"Either start working, start reading, or get out of the library. This isn't a halfway house."

I helped Mrs. Berns off the floor. "This might be a good time to introduce you two. Mrs. Berns, this is Sarah Ruth. She's going to run the library when I leave."

"You ain't leaving."

I sighed. This was an argument I couldn't win. "Sarah Ruth, Mrs. Berns. Mrs. Berns, Sarah Ruth."

Sarah Ruth chuckled. "It was nice to meet you, Mrs. Berns. I look forward to starting work with you on Monday."

"If I come. My social calendar fills pretty quick, you know." With that, Mrs. Berns went back to shelving books. No more farts, fake cat feces, or gunshots. I took that to mean she liked her new boss. I walked Sarah Ruth out into the blazing heat of the early afternoon, wondering at the squishiness of the molten pavement.

"It's a good summer to own a lake home," I offered.

"Yes, I love it."

I smiled politely. My comment had been general, but her response had been specific. When Sarah Ruth got into her car, I returned to the air-conditioned coolness of the library and breathed deeply. Then, I tracked down Mrs. Berns in the reference section, where she was looking up "thespian."

"Huhn. I always thought it was one of those women who like women. Guess Ida wins that bet."

"Sarah Ruth seems nice."

"Humph. If you like those gangly, pear-shaped women with pizzly home perms. Mostly, that type's just good for childbearing, but if you think she can be a librarian, then what do I know?"

"Maybe she's like olives."

"Huh?"

"Olives. When I was a kid, I wanted to like olives, and I wanted a retainer. Don't ask me why. So I forced down green and black olives until I could stomach them, and I sucked on grape Jolly Ranchers until they fit in the roof of my mouth to pretend like I had a retainer."

"If you're trying to convince me we're better off without you here, you're on the right train."

"I outgrew wanting the retainer, but I ended up liking olives. Green ones, at least. Maybe Sarah Ruth is like an olive—you just have to work to like her."

"What's in it for me?"

I blinked, hard, and turned to the back room. "I'm going to get our new shipment catalogued. You know where to find me if anyone needs me."

I'm pretty sure I heard a muttered, "Chickenshit," as I strode to the back, but it was too quiet to be certain. It could have just been my conscience.

ABOUT THE AUTHOR

Jess Lourey spent her formative years in Paynesville, Minnesota, a small town not unlike the *Murder-by-Month* series' Battle Lake. She teaches English and sociology full time at a two-year college. When not raising her wonderful kids, teaching, or writing, you can find her gardening and navigating the niceties and meanities of small-town life. She is a member of Mystery Writers of America, Sisters in Crime, the Loft, and Lake Superior Writers.